KILL HER IF YOU CAN

THE CLASSIC HANK JANSON

The first original Hank Janson book appeared in 1946, and the last in 1971. However, the classic era on which we are focusing in the Telos reissue series lasted from 1946 to 1953. The following is a checklist of those books, which were subdivided into five main series and a number of 'specials'.

PRE-SERIES BOOKS
When Dames Get Tough (1946)
Scarred Faces (1947)

SERIES ONE
1) This Woman Is Death (1948)
2) Lady, Mind That Corpse (1948)
3) Gun Moll For Hire (1948)
4) No Regrets For Clara (194)
5) Smart Girls Don't Talk (1949)
6) Lilies For My Lovely (1949)
7) Blonde On The Spot (1949)
8) Honey, Take My Gun (1949)
9) Sweetheart, Here's Your Grave (1949)
10) Gunsmoke In Her Eyes (1949)
11) Angel, Shoot To Kill (1949)
12) Slay-Ride For Cutie (1949)

SERIES TWO
13) Sister, Don't Hate Me (1949)
14) Some Look Better Dead (1950)
15) Sweetie, Hold Me Tight (1950)
16) Torment For Trixie (1950)
17) Don't Dare Me, Sugar (1950)
18) The Lady Has A Scar (1950)
19) The Jane With The Green Eyes (1950)
20) Lola Brought Her Wreath (1950)
21) Lady, Toll The Bell (1950)
22) The Bride Wore Weeds (1950)
23) Don't Mourn Me Toots (1951)
24) This Dame Dies Soon (1951)

SERIES THREE
25) Baby, Don't Dare Squeal (1951)
26) Death Wore A Petticoat (1951)
27) Hotsy, You'll Be Chilled (1951)

28) It's Always Eve That Weeps (1951)
29) Frails Can Be So Tough (1951)
30) Milady Took The Rap (1951)
31) Women Hate Till Death (1951)
32) Broads Don't Scare Easy (1951)
33) Skirts Bring Me Sorrow (1951)
34) Sadie Don't Cry Now (1952)
35) The Filly Wore A Rod (1952)
36) Kill Her If You Can (1952)

SERIES FOUR
37) Murder (1952)
38) Conflict (1952)
39) Tension (1952)
40) Whiplash (1952)
41) Accused (1952)
42) Killer (1952)
43) Suspense (1952)
44) Pursuit (1953)
45) Vengeance (1953)
46) Torment (1953)
47) Amok (1953)
48) Corruption (1953)

SERIES FIVE
49) Silken Menace (1953)
50) Nyloned Avenger (1953)

SPECIALS
Auctioned (1952)
Persian Pride (1952)
Desert Fury (1953)
One Man In His Time (1953)
Unseen Assassin (1953)
Deadly Mission (1953)

KILL HER IF YOU CAN

HANK JANSON

This edition first published in England in 2005 by
Telos Publishing Ltd
5A Church Road, Shortlands, Bromley, Kent, BR2 0HP,
United Kingdom

www.telos.co.uk

Telos Publishing Ltd values feedback. Please e-mail us with any
comments you may have about this book to: feedback@telos.co.uk

ISBN: 978-1-84583-961-1

This edition © 2017 Telos Publishing Ltd
Introduction © 2005 Steve Holland

Novel by Stephen D Frances
Cover by Reginald Heade
With thanks to Steve Holland
www.hankjanson.co.uk
Silhouette device by Philip Mendoza
Cover design by David J Howe

The Hank Janson name, logo and silhouette device are registered
trademarks of Telos Publishing Ltd

First published in England by New Fiction Press, March 1952

British Library Cataloguing in Publication Data.
A catalogue record for this book is available from the British Library.

PUBLISHER'S NOTE

The appeal of the Hank Janson books to a modern readership lies not only in the quality of the storytelling, which is as powerfully compelling today as it was when they were first published, but also in the fascinating insight they afford into the attitudes, customs and morals of the 1940s and 1950s. We have therefore endeavoured to make *Kill Her If You Can*, and all our other Hank Janson reissues, as faithful to the original editions as possible. Unlike some other publishers, who when reissuing vintage fiction have been known edit it to remove aspects that might offend present-day sensibilities, we have left the original narrative absolutely intact.

The original editions of these classic Hank Janson titles made quite frequent use of phonetic 'Americanisms' such as 'kinda', 'gotta', 'wanna' and so on. Again, we have left these unchanged in the Telos Publishing Ltd reissues, to give readers as genuine as possible a taste of what it was like to read these books when they first came out, even though such devices have since become sorta out of fashion.

The only way in which we have amended the original text has been to correct obvious lapses in spelling, grammar and punctuation, and to remedy clear typesetting errors.

Lastly, we should mention that we have made every effort to trace and acquire relevant copyrights in the various elements that make up this book. However, if anyone has any further information that they could provide in this regard, we would be very grateful to receive it.

INTRODUCTION

Kill Her If You Can was the thirty-sixth Janson novel and historic in a minor way. It was the twelfth and final novel in the third Janson series, published in March 1952, and marked the end of one of the most troubled periods of Janson's history.

As the Hank Janson novels began to gain popularity, Stephen Frances, their author and publisher, had holidayed in Spain in the late 1940s and found himself in the delightful village of Rosas on the Costa Brava. Over the next couple of years, Frances visited the village again and decided to buy an apartment to escape from rationing and the grey austerity of post-war London. In 1950 he had made the acquaintance of printer's rep Reginald Herbert Carter, and the two had become firm friends. Carter had ambitions as a publisher and offered to take over the Janson novels, freeing Frances of the day-to-day grind of chasing paper supplies, dealing with printers, and the dozens of other tasks that went into getting the Janson books onto the newsagent's shelves.

The agreement Frances had reached with Reg Carter meant that all rights to the Janson name were taken over by Carter and his new company, New Fiction Press, an imprint of Editions Poetry (London) Ltd, which Carter had purchased in August 1951. Carter and Julius Reiter, whose Gaywood Press were the sole distributors of the Janson novels, set up a printing company, and Carter purchased a second company, Comyns Ltd., to begin publishing further gangster thrillers alongside the Jansons.

At the same time, Frances's personal life was in upheaval; his marriage had failed and his mother was diagnosed with cancer. The latter died in November 1951, and Frances decided that there was now no reason to stay in England permanently.

Against this background, Frances still had to keep turning out novels. 'Published by S D Frances' disappeared from the title page to be replaced by 'Published by New Fiction Press' on the novel *Frails Can Be So Tough*. More dramatically, the beautifully painted cover by Reginald (Heade) Webb also disappeared. A few months earlier, Archer Press had been heavily fined for publishing three 'obscene' novels, all of which had Heade covers; the Hank Janson novel *Gunsmoke In Her Eyes* had also been the cause of a fine levelled against a bookseller in Blackburn.

Three artwork covers disappeared entirely, replaced by a silhouette of Hank. Two more were sent back through the printing presses so that the 'dame' depicted on the cover could be obscured by silver ink. The next was slightly repainted to make it less revealing. The seventh, that for *The Filly Wore a Rod*, was replaced entirely. That for *Kill Her If You Can*, the next book in sequence, was, as far as I am aware, painted at the same time (probably during the autumn of 1951) as the published cover for *The Filly Wore A Rod* – the title lettering and 2/- cover price make this obvious.[1]

With all this activity, personal and professional, affecting Frances, it is little wonder that the Hank Janson novels published around that time were of somewhat shaky quality. *Kill Her If You Can* is a generic crime thriller set around the premise of an unknown assailant's attempts to assassinate a wealthy heiress. Because of the generic nature of the Hank Janson titles, it could as easily have appeared under the title

---

[1] The original painted covers for *Broads Don't Scare Easy* and *Skirts Bring Me Sorrow* have been used on the Telos reissue editions, both of which were originally to have been priced at 1/6.

Broads Don't Scare Easy, or *Frails Can Be So Tough*, or *Skirts Bring Me Sorrow* ... Frances chose the titles for the simple reason that the covers were prepared long in advance of the story being written. This also explains why there is a blonde on the cover, while Beryl Pinder, the endangered heiress, has 'bluey-black' hair.

Whilst *Kill Her If You Can* is a relatively unremarkable Janson novel, plot-wise, it does contain quite a few interesting insights into Janson, the character, and his author.

The story told to Hank by a barman early in the novel – that Russian peasants were eating babies to ward off starvation – was the kind of McCarthyist propaganda that was circulating in America at the time. Frances, a former Communist himself, had a firm idea of how the Cold War was being sustained by fear of 'The Red Menace'. The Rosenberg atomic spy case was big news in 1951, Julius and Ethel Rosenberg having been arrested in 1950 for persuading Ethel's brother, who worked at Los Alamos, to reveal classified data on nuclear weapons, which were then passed to the Soviet Union. Frances's passing mention of Albania, then in the grip of radical political upheaval as Enver

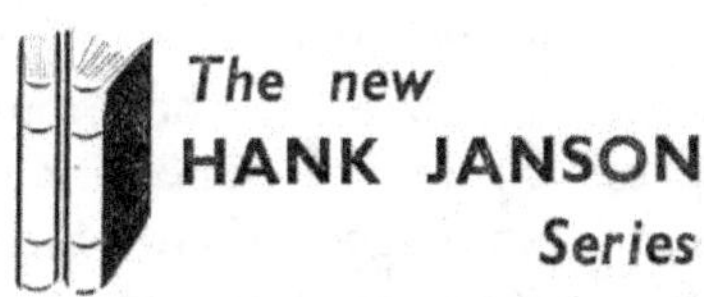

An advertisement for the next series of Hank Janson books was printed at the back of *Kill Her If You Can*.

Hoxha secured power by a Stalinist purge of his enemies, shows that he had not lost his interest in European politics.

Although by 1951 Frances had become less politically active, he still maintained a fierce personal philosophy, and he continued to attack injustice and name those whom he saw as the guilty parties through the voice of Hank Janson. In *Kill Her If You Can,* the plot stalled half way through the first chapter while Frances issued a polemic against the media.

The real hope of civilisation is that ordinary folk, the quiet, ordinary folk, won't be herded beyond the limits of reasonableness by the ferocity of printed and broadcast propaganda when the pressure is put on and is intended to whip the peoples of the world into red-hot, suicidal war fervour.

As well as attacking government-sponsored paranoia, Frances also ground his heel into the police with a brief but bitter description of police interrogation tactics. All in the space of ten pages, after which Frances allows himself a breather to get on with the story. Our endangered heiress, Beryl Pinder, turns out to be something of a spitfire as she snaps and sneers out her answers to the police, denying any knowledge about why she would be a bomber's target. Frances cleverly shows how Beryl tries to control the situation, The cops are outside the circle of light they use during the interrogation; Beryl is the focus of their rapt attention, drawing them in, asking for a cigarette, crossing her legs, mocking the officers… Think Sharon Stone in *Basic Instinct.*

In places, Frances allows humour or a pressing need to inform the reader to suspend the plot, not always to the benefit of the novel. Having written sixty novels by this time, he was usually a little less obvious with his padding, but scenes between an American and a British pilot at a Flying Club visited by Hank and a brief history of women's clothing smack of space filler material. Elsewhere, Frances can nail a scene or character in a few lines:

She smoked like a man. Without removing the

cigarette from her mouth she said, 'Can't *you* fill in all this nonsense about security number and so on?' The cigarette bobbed between her lips as she spoke.

Frances uses his descriptions to good effect. The setting was America, and slipping in a phrase like 'The guy behind the huge oak desk who was obviously the apartment manager, was dressed like a Fifth Avenue tailor's advertisement' helped convince his readership that Hank was the genuine article. He occasionally slips: 'stinks department' (for forensics) is, I'm sure, British (meaning chemistry department); the later use of 'four-flusher' (a cheat or swindler) would have been more acceptable in a Western and is used wrongly (the context implies Beryl is saying Janson is useless or, perhaps, even a coward). But for the most part Frances sells Hank convincingly.

The best aspect of *Kill Her If You Can* is the relationship between Hank and Beryl, the plot being almost incidental. The last third of the novel is a fine example of Frances's ability to wrench the most out of a situation. Hank and Beryl make their way to an isolated shack in the middle of nowhere, and the already tense relationship between Janson and the headstrong Beryl boils over under the merciless sun. The description of what happens when Beryl's attacker tracks them down and the gruelling, nightmarish aftermath as the two walk to the nearest town sixty miles away is Frances at his finest.

Steve Holland
Colchester, September 2004.

KILL HER IF YOU CAN

1

It's happened in Albania, it's happened once or twice in Britain, and in some small countries in Europe it's probably a common-day occurrence.

But it isn't common in America!

And since the days of prohibition, it hasn't been common in Chicago!

But it's said there's nothing new under the sun, and I guess Chicago was just as likely a place for it to happen as in Moscow or Paris.

I got the tip-off from an excited member of the public who shouted so loudly through the phone on account of his ringing ear-drums that I had to ask the address three times before I could understand it.

It took three-quarters of an hour to get there on account of the traffic held up for blocks around, and by that time the cops had everything in hand, had cordoned off the whole block and were hugely enjoying themselves like this was a police gala day.

From the outside of the apartment block it didn't look like anything had happened except for the four crimson fire engines, the two white ambulances and the half-a-dozen black squad cars. There was a little glass scattered in the roadway but nothing to attract special attention.

There were so many officious cops around wanting me to flash my press card that I carried it in my hand, breast high, so they didn't have to ask for it.

Yeah, it looked like a gala day for the cops, the Fire Department and the Red Cross as well. The entrance lounge to the apartment block was packed thick with them. Once inside the lobby, I could see further evidence of the explosion. Plaster had fallen from the ceiling and was trodden into the thick, luxurious carpet by cops' large number nines, dust was floating in the air like an invisible cloud and tickling the back of my throat, while the sharp tang of cordite irritated my nostrils.

Things had been quiet in town during the past coupla weeks. Maybe that explained the zealousness of the Fire Department, who'd unrolled a coupla miles of hosepipes and run them in through the lobby and up the stairs.

There was no fire that I could see. Not even a wreath of smoke. Maybe that explained the slightly crestfallen faces of the firemen.

There was more evidence as I climbed the stairs to the first floor. Plaster had fallen from the ceiling in thick lumps, powdered the stairway and scrunched underfoot as I shouldered my way through the mass of uniforms. I couldn't have encountered more brass and uniforms if I'd been at Regimental Headquarters.

The explosion had taken place on the first floor. When I reached it, there wasn't any doubting where it'd happened. Plaster had been shaken from the walls of the corridors, leaving them stripped and showing the naked brickwork beneath. Half the apartment doors were open, hanging crazily from broken hinges, splintered so that sharp tongues of white, jagged wood speared at my eyes.

The explosion had taken place in apartment Ten. There wasn't much doubt about that either. I didn't have to open the door to see into apartment number Ten. I didn't have to do anything except stumble over loose brickwork in order to stare into the apartment and see it in perspective like a dolls house when roof and front have been removed.

It musta been quite an explosion. This was a new apartment block, modern and strongly made, expensive to rent.

It musta been nicely furnished too. But I couldn't bet on it. A coupla tons of brickwork, plaster and ceiling distributed around can make a room or flat awful untidy and dusty.

Sid Walker, the *Chronicle's* photographer, was down on one knee beside me, firing his flashlight as fast as he could insert new films. I carefully studied the scene, noted everything worthy of interest, and when Sid nodded at me with satisfaction, I threaded my way back along the corridor and downstairs to the entrance hall.

Maybe most folks don't know it, but to a reporter it's commonplace. Whenever anything happens it's always terribly difficult to find out *exactly* what has happened.

There were dozens of folks around, cops, firemen, and residents. All of them, even the cops, were anxious to be helpful. I had more than a dozen around me, volunteering information, keeping an hopeful eye on Sid Walker and hoping I'd be lining them up to take their photos as '*eye witness of the explosion.*'

Yeah, there were a coupla dozen of them eager and anxious to give me information. The trouble was, none of them knew anything beyond that there'd been a '*big bang.*' Any minor detailed information they gave was contradicted among themselves.

Being a reporter, you get used to that kinda thing. When there's a road accident, one guy says the injured party ran across in front of the truck, a second guy says the truck swerved into the kerb and hit the injured party, while a third guy saw a private car (which no-one else saw) cause the truck to swerve onto the wrong side of the road, and a fourth guy says nothing of the kind happened, that the injured party tripped and fell and the truck driver never touched him.

It's no use the reporter going to work on the truck driver. He's usually a bundle of nerves, scared out of his life he's killed someone, worried sick what will happen to his wife and kids if he gets jail, and worriedly thinking the best he can hope for is the sack.

The injured party isn't going to give you much assistance either. Because if by this time he isn't injected with morphia or too dazed with pain to be asked questions, he'll have his lawyer squatting beside him.

There are lawyers known as accident vultures. They're like desert vultures, can scent an accident almost before it's happened, are drawn to the scene of the accident by some strange sixth sense, which leads them unerringly to their prey. Almost before a crowd has begun to gather and the harness cop on the street corner has begun his ponderous, loping stride towards the accident, the lawyer vulture is cradling the injured party's head on his knee, while he unscrews his fountain pen and produces a form giving the lawyer power of attorney to negotiate and obtain damages on behalf of the injured man.

When the injured party has one of those legal eagles sitting beside him, you can't get a word out of him. The legal bandit won't let you get a word out of him. Anything whatsoever that is said may be produced as evidence. The lawyer isn't willing any evidence shall be produced until every link in the testimony has been carefully tested for its strength and ability to produce extensive damages, of which – needless to say – the injured person may obtain a little after paying the expenses of the lawyer.

There weren't any lawyers around that apartment, for a reason that I discovered later. But the lawyers' absence didn't help me any. I still wasn't getting any worthwhile facts.

I caught Sid Walker's eye, nodded my head towards the door and managed to tear myself away from the voluble eye-witnesses who'd seen nothing and wanted to tell me all about it. I took Sid on one side, lit a cigarette, said thoughtfully: 'Better make this a picture spread, Sid. There's a story somewhere, but it's deep down. Get back to the office quick, get those shots printed and spread them on the front page. Tell the Chief to label it *"Mystery Explosion"*.'

'Aren't you coming back, Hank?'

'I'll stick around,' I said. 'I'll dig down a little, find out how deep this goes.'

I stuck around.

So did twelve other reporters. It didn't do us any good. Plenty of folk were willing to tell us about the loud explosion, the windows splintering into fragments, the trembling floor and the vibration of it as plaster was cracking and splitting from walls and ceilings.

But there wasn't one guy who could tell me what caused the explosion!

There wasn't one guy who could tell me who, if anyone, had been in that apartment when the explosion took place!

It was the dust in the air that gave me my thirst. I quit after an hour, found myself a bar with bright red, leather-covered high-stools, twined my legs around the long, chromium-plated tubular legs as I gratefully moistened my dry mouth with ice-cold lager.

The bartender eyed my suit, which was soiled from plaster and dust, asked inquisitively: 'Were you anywhere near the explosion on 47th?'

'I arrived later,' I told him.

'Yeah!' He suddenly wasn't so affable, was suddenly cold and distant.

I put down my empty glass, gestured for a refill. As he gave me my change, he said knowingly: 'Cop, huh?'

'Way off mark,' I replied. 'Reporter.'

He lost his distant, cold aloofness, thawed visibly, rested his elbows on the counter.

'One helluva explosion,' he told me. 'Rattled the glasses on my shelves.' He leaned farther forward across the counter, lowered his voice conspiratorially. 'You figure it really was them fellas? Seems like there's nothing they won't do.'

'What fellas?' I asked sharply.

'Them Kremlin guys,' he said. 'They say as how they've got cells all over, a vast spy ring. Not proper Russians either. Just ordinary fellas like you and me, just plain ordinary Americans who've been fed a lotta propaganda. I've heard they're gonna blow up all the public statues, and city halls. There's a fifth column in Chicago big enough to be a sixth, seventh and eighth column as well.'

'You've got it all figured, Bud,' I said. 'I can tell right off you're a clear-thinking, logical, American citizen.'

'Sure thing,' he said with pleasure. 'Plain as the nose on your face. This is the start of it. Pretty soon they'll blow up the power houses and the arms depots. Then where shall we be?'

'You tell me,' I suggested.

'Right in the thick of it,' he said, leaning over the counter towards me, jaw jutting and eyes glowing. 'Why from what I hear, there ain't nothing those guys won't do.'

I took another deep draft of beer. 'I once heard,' I informed him, 'that when they're short of grub in Russia, they round up the new-born babies, share them among the starving peasants to ward off the famine. They say there's parts of Russia where the peasants have never eaten any other kind of meat.'

There was the faintest gleam of doubt in his eyes. 'It ain't likely that would happen here. Not with Americans.'

'You never can tell,' I said solemnly, and finished my beer.

He thought it over. He said slowly, like he was still chewing over what I'd said and was finding it a tasty morsel of news, 'Why d'you figure they use babies? Why not the bigger kids.'

I stared at him solemnly. 'Can't you figure that for yourself?'

He was leaning right across the counter now, jaw jutting and eyes glowing fanatically.

'Seems to me like the big kids might go around farther.'

'But the bigger children can be worked,' I explained. 'They can be harnessed to ploughs, lashed 'til they drop from exhaustion. Besides...' I paused dramatically, and his eyes glowed hungrily, his fanatical mind eager for a fresh tit-bit.

'Besides ...,' I said, '... the flesh of a baby is more... tender!'

This is the middle of the 20th Century. This is the age of the word. Not the word of brotherly love, as advocated two thousand years ago by a simple fisherman, but the age of the printed and spoken word.

Never before in history have the words of prominent men been so forced upon simple peoples of the world. Spoken words are hurled through the ether, hammered again and again at peace-loving folk who want nothing other than to go on being peace loving.

The ordinary guy can't get away from those words. The crackling radio news voice follows him to the ends of the world, the printed page carries its large quota of politicians' statements, and the ordinary man sitting at home in his stockinged feet, relaxing after a hard day's work, is shocked and worried, made to feel he is living on the knife-edge of atomic destruction as the battle of the ether is waged unceasingly and emerges from his loudspeaker in the form of news broadcasts.

Politicians consider themselves pretty important guys. Maybe they get that way on account of talking so much about themselves, while talking themselves into the House of Representatives.

But no matter how important they think themselves, they know they can't run wars without help. They need the help of the ordinary folk to wage war.

Hitler once needed the help of ordinary folk. He set a new fashion in politics. He discovered the way to ensure obtaining the help of the ordinary folk was, to use his own words: *'The printed word and the broadcast word. The lie. The thumping big lie, repeated again and again, hammered at the nation by the radio and the press, repeated ceaselessly until a whole nation believes the unbelievable.'*

Yeah, Hitler set a new fashion for politicians, and he chose the eve of the discovery of the atom bomb to make his offering to the Gods of Mars. The lie, the half-lie and the half-truth as well as the truth can and are now used unceasingly to keep the ordinary folk of all the world dangling in suspense. All of them! *All* the quiet, ordinary folk of *all* the countries of the world are lectured and instructed, warned and persuaded, worked on by propaganda in every manner known to radio and printing.

While all they want is to live in peace!

It's a tremendous snowball of words. The fear of war is spread, military service becomes compulsory. Home guards are enrolled, blood donors are registered, pilots are trained, chemists and scientists are working overtime and the quiet, ordinary folk of all countries are on the threshold of disaster, about to plunge into the final struggle between nations, knowing full well that in this atomic age the forces of destruction, once unleashed, will be too powerful for anyone to control.

Knowing full well that when that war ends, there will be nothing but lifeless devastation.

Knowing this is universal suicide!

Being a reporter gives you an objective view on life. You get used to being apart from the crowd and watching folk working, thinking and throbbing with life.

Maybe I've got the wrong angle. Maybe the quiet, ordinary folk don't feel the way I think they do. Maybe they ain't so quiet, maybe they wanna be talked into war.

If so. I'm wrong.

But this jutting-jawed bartender with glowing, fanatical eyes symbolized my impressions. This is the middle of the 20th Century, the atomic age when religious organisations have finally agreed that their followers are not obliged to believe in Hell, when even fanciful folk no longer believe in ghosts, and when the law no longer recognises evidence proving a woman is a witch.

Yet here was a guy whose mind had been conditioned by the radio and the press to believe almost anything bad said or written about a certain country.

I believe there's a whole lotta things wrong in Russia. I believe there's a whole lotta things wrong in the whole of this topsy-turvy world.

But the real hope for civilisation is that ordinary folk, the quiet, ordinary folk, won't be herded beyond the limits of reasonableness by the ferocity of printed and broadcast propaganda when the pressure is put on and is intended to whip the peoples of the world into red-hot, suicidal war fervour.

I pushed my glass across the counter, stood up, lit a cigarette.

'I figure there's nothing them bastards wouldn't do,' he said, eyes glowing angrily.

'Listen, pal,' I said quietly. 'I don't know what kinda cereals you take for breakfast, but you oughta take more salt with them.'

There was that glint of suspicion in his eyes again. 'Say,' he rasped. 'Who's side you on anyway?'

'The only side that matters,' I told him. 'The side of you and me and the rest of humanity.'

The suspicion in his eyes heightened, his lips curled in a sneer. 'That's just the way it's done,' he mouthed. 'It's just the way you Reds do it, worm yourself into a guy's confidence, suck him dry and pass on the information to an agent so it goes back to Moscow.'

'Thanks for the tip about the explosion,' I told him. 'It's useful to know who really did it.'

'You! A reporter!' he sneered disbelievingly. 'You're a fifth columnist. Maybe I ought to call the cops now.'

'There's one thing you oughta do for sure,' I told him.

The glowing eyes were suspicious but curious. 'Yeah? What's that?'

'Stop reading the papers,' I told him.

I went back to the apartment block. It was still cordoned off, still overrun by uniforms. I used different tactics this time, ignored the dicks and the Army brass examining the ruins for evidence of sabotage, and finally ran to earth the manager of the block, who lived in the penthouse on the roof.

He was a podgy guy with fat hands, bald head, watery blue eyes and a habit of putting his fist against his mouth to cover the discreet little cough that prefaced everything he said.

He opened up the door of his snug little flat, eyed me with an air of resignation. Then he coughed against his fist, said wearily: 'More questions, I suppose?'

It wasn't the first time I'd been mistaken for a cop. I let it ride. 'Just a few more,' I said.

He opened the door bleakly, invited me into a midget-sized lounge. I didn't take the seat he offered, instead stood with feet astride, rocking back on my heels and eyeing him piercingly. 'What's the name of the party who rents that flat?'

He coughed against his fist. 'How many more times?' he sighed. 'I musta told it a dozen times.' He sighed again. 'Beryl Pinder.'

'Did she live alone?'

He nodded. 'Sure. New tenant. Been here about a month.'

'Where was she when it happened?'

He looked up at me sharply, coughed against his hand. 'Say, you fellas must be disorganzied. You've got her down at headquarters. You oughta know better than me.'

'Just answer the questions,' I said grimly. 'Where was she when it happened?'

He shrugged his shoulders, coughed. 'All I know is what she told me. She was just entering the building when it happened.'

'How long had she been out?'

There was a sharp suspicion in his watery eyes. 'I've only got her word for it,' he said. 'The same as she told you people. Three or four hours.'

'Can you confirm that?'

The discreet cough. 'I've told you guys again and again. All I know is that an hour before the explosion, a registered parcel arrived for her. The postman couldn't deliver it, couldn't get a reply, so he brought it down to the commissionaire. The commissionaire signed for it, took it up to her apartment, left it on her table, using the master key. She wasn't in the apartment then. That's all I can tell you.'

'Where's the commissionaire?' I said, 'I wanna talk with him.'

The suspicion in his eyes was strong now. This time he didn't cough against the back of his hand. 'Now wait a minute,' he said slowly. 'Just what kinda cop are you anyway?

You've had my commissionaire down at headquarters for more than an hour. Now you're here asking me where he is. I'm getting kinda sick of all this. On top of it, I've got dozens of tenants on my heels, asking when the repairs are gonna be done, asking me for this and ...'

'Cut it,' I snarled. 'I don't wanna hear about your worries. Who were the eye-witnesses near enough to see what happened?'

He took a deep breath, sighed with delicate impatience, gestured expressively with his podgy hands. 'Say, fella. Why don't you go back down headquarters. Seems like everyone you wanna talk to is right there.'

I glared at him.

He glared back.

I took a deep breath, thrust my hands deep into my pockets. 'Okay,' I growled sullenly. 'I guess that's all.' He stood at the door of his apartment and watched me as I made my way downstairs. There was bewilderment as well as suspicion in his watery blue eyes.

2

To be a good reporter, you have to be in well with the cops. And as in all other walks of life, there are good cops and bad cops. That's why I'm not such a good reporter as I might be. I don't get on so well with the bad cops.

But I was in luck. I made enquiries at headquarters, learned that Inspector Blunt was in charge of the case. That was fine and dandy, because Blunt's a good cop, an honest cop, and by way of being a friend of mine.

I spoke to cop Sergeants, argued with their superior officers and finally made them obtain telephone permission from Blunt for me to join him in the sweat room.

The sweat room's where the cops get most of their information. And that's the place where you can tell the difference between good cops and bad cops.

The good cop uses psychology on the suspect being cross-examined under the strong, white arc lamps.

The bad cop locks himself in with the suspect and two broad-shouldered dicks, and none of them emerges until the suspect has volunteered information. During the course of such an interview, it frequently occurs that the suspect accidentally falls off his chair. That's supposed to explain how he gets the blue welts that bruise his flesh from his neck to the base of the spine and cause him to arch with pain. That's supposed to explain the blood on the floor, the pulped nose, the discoloured eye and puffed lips.

It doesn't, of course. But then, who worries about a guy who is caught red-handed and is a known criminal? And, anyway, by the time he comes up for trial, bruises will have disappeared.

Blunt was a good cop. The sweat room door wasn't locked! I sidled inside unobtrusively, leaned against the shadowed, whitewashed wall and peered through the cigarette smoke at the dame sitting on the solitary chair centered beneath the strong, white, burning glare of a naked, high-voltage electric bulb.

Blunt was standing facing her just outside the circle of fierce white light projected downwards by the lamp. His face was shadowy, his figure a dark silhouette. Other hard-faced, shadowy figures stood around staring at the dame intently.

She was a proud dame. I could see that right away. At the same time, I saw lots of other things. She wasn't scared. Not one tiny bit! On the contrary, she was hopping mad, Infuriated and dangerously angry, but clever enough to keep herself under control.

That pitiless light probed her face mercilessly, and she was good for the test. Her skin was flawless, although the strong light made her appear pale. She wasn't pretty! That's a word you'd use to describe the attractive, chocolate-box face of a chorus girl. No, she wasn't pretty. But she just missed being beautiful. She had a kinda hard, set, determined, dignified and proud face that right away made me wanna keep looking at her.

She hadn't the pert-faced, peroxided-hair and bright red cupid-bow lips beauty. Instead she had the serene, haughty beauty of a queen, the self-confidence of a determined woman and the irresistible fascination always exuded by a charming dame who is the mental equal of her menfolk.

She was attractive and she was feminine, and she had to be to earn my attention in the get-up she was wearing. She wore tight blue jeans that clung tightly to her smooth thighs and failed to reach her ankles by three or four inches. She also wore canary-yellow socks and flat-heeled brogues. Her hair was a kinda bluey-black, a gleaming silky texture that was wind-blown, dishevelled and long enough to brush the shoulders of her windjammer. It was hot in that room. That was one reason why she'd opened up her windjammer. The other reason coulda been that, with typical feminine greed for admiration, she wanted to demonstrate how well she could fill a sweater. She was good at it. She could do it at least as well as anyone I'd ever met. It was a yellow sweater, tight-fitting in the right places and loose enough in other places to give full emphasis to her considerable feminine charms.

Blunt said stonily, his voice sounding harsh and staccato in that hot, dried-up atmosphere, 'And you don't know anyone who would send such a parcel?'

She eyed him levelly, said with a dangerous quietness: 'I've told you that six times.'

'I'm sorry that you don't approve of our methods, Miss Pinder,' said Blunt, with grim irony. 'But you must leave us to be the judge of that. How many times we ask the same question is a matter for us to decide.'

Her eyes flashed. 'And I'm supposed to sit here answering the same stupid questions over and over again?'

Blunt breathed deeply. 'Listen, Miss Pinder,' he said, seriously. 'It was lucky the explosion injured no-one. But it might have killed several people.' He paused a moment, said with emphasis: 'It might even have killed you.'

'You're scaring the life outta me,' she sneered.

'My job is to find out all I can and prevent other innocent people being involved in a similar incident.'

'Okay, okay,' she snapped. 'So a parcel arrived for me containing a bomb. I don't know who sent it or why it should have been addressed to me. I didn't even know it was in my apartment. What more can I tell you? Who are you trying to drive nuts, yourself or me? Where does it get you, asking the same questions over and over again?'

'But *someone* sent you that parcel,' insisted Blunt. '*Someone* knew your name, knew your address, sent that parcel by registered post with a time-bomb inside, having carefully calculated it wouldn't explode until after it had passed through the mails.'

She clenched her fists in aggravation, raised her eyes despairingly to heaven. 'Holy smoke,' she breathed wearily. 'Over and over again. The same words, the same intonation.' Then she flared at him again. 'What more can I do? What more can I tell you? You want I should tell lies? You want I should invent something? Will that make you happy?'

Blunt said slowly: 'I'm afraid, Miss Pinder, you don't seem to realize the seriousness of what has happened. I should like to make it ...'

'Gimme a cigarette,' she commanded.

Blunt's teeth clicked together, he breathed hard and stared at the dame challengingly.

She stared back, her long lashes wide apart, her hazel-coloured eyes insolently meeting his challenge.

Blunt made an impatient gesture. One of the dicks stepped forward into the circle of light, extended a packet of cigarettes, thumbed his cigarette-lighter into life and held it for her.

She took a slow, grateful drag at the cigarette, slumped back lazily in her chair, looped one thumb in the waistband of her jeans and crossed her legs. Then, with sugary, mockingly polite intonation, she said: 'What was it you were saying?'

It took a lot to rattle Blunt. He said quietly: 'I was about to point out, Miss Pinder, that you do not apparently realize the seriousness of your situation. A brown paper parcel, containing a time-bomb, was sent through the mails. If there'd been a premature explosion, the lives of many post-office workers might have been lost. The sender of that parcel must be found and found quickly before there's a repetition of what's happened.'

'Okay, Inspector,' she drawled. 'Get busy. Do something. You've got my best wishes. I don't want another of those parcels popping through my letter-box.'

Blunt's jaw was like iron. 'We're getting busy, Miss Pinder,' he said icily. 'So far, we've got only one link, apart from a few tattered pieces of brown paper and the remnants of the timing mechanism.'

She stared at him, interest in her eyes. Blunt elaborated his statement and her curiosity got the better of her. 'Yeah, what's that?'

'We've got *you*,' he said quietly.

His words shocked her. Momentarily her face became wooden, her cigarette remained suspended in the air halfway towards her lips. It stopped that way for seconds. Then fury gleamed in her eyes. She hurled the cigarette across the room, leaped to her feet, strode across to Blunt, stood staring up into his face, trembling with rage and hands clenched tightly at her sides. 'Why, you great, flat-footed brute,' she gritted. 'You half-witted corpse collector. Are you crazy enough to suggest I sent myself that bomb? Are you so stupid ...?'

One of the dicks moved in close, tapped her gently on the shoulder, said with a note of command in his voice: 'Sit down, lady.'

She flared around at him, knocked his arm to one side. 'Take your dirty hands off me, you slimy snoop hound.'

The dick stepped back quickly, startled, his cheeks slowly reddening with suppressed anger.

Blunt said in a hard voice: 'I'm trying to be reasonable, Miss Pinder. This is no way for ...'

She rounded on Blunt again, eyes flaming, her slight figure trembling with anger. 'Reasonable! Reasonable!! REASONABLE!!! You keep me here for an hour asking the same stupid questions and finally accuse me of sending myself a bomb. Reasonable! Is there anything about this cock-eyed police force that can possibly be called reasonable?'

The red-faced dick was tapping her on the shoulder again 'Siddown, lady,' he growled. 'Siddown.'

'This bunch of morons you've got here ought to have their hands tied behind their backs,' she flared at Blunt. 'You're not cops, you're cutie-cuddlers. Anything to get your hands on a dame. Asking crazy ...'

The red-faced dick was more determined. He took her firmly by the shoulders. 'I said siddown, lady,' he growled.

She may have been slight, but she was strong and wiry. She twisted from his big hands like an eel, spun around quicker than the eye could follow, and as the sharp crack of her palm against his cheek echoed around the room, he staggered back, face even redder than it had been before. 'Just a minute,' said Blunt suddenly angry. 'You can't treat my men like that. Now just you ...'

Blunt made the same mistake as the dick. He took the girl by the shoulder, intended to steer her towards the chair. Her palm slapped with the speed of the forked tongue of a snake. Blunt rocked back on his heels, shocked surprise in his eyes as his left hand went up to his smarting cheek.

'No one's gonna push me around,' she stormed angrily. 'And while I'm about it ...'

She lunged angrily towards another dick. He was luckier, realized her intentions, managed to parry her swinging arm and instinctively and defensively moved in on her, wrapped his arms around her waist.

Until that moment, she'd been a contentedly sleeping cat compared with what she now became. She was an enraged tigress, spitting, tearing with her nails, kicking, biting and butting with her head.

She was magnificent!

I stood back and admired her. I didn't have to do anything about her, so it was easy for me. But it wasn't so easy for the dicks. It was three or four minutes before they got her under control with arms firmly held behind her. And by then, not one dick hadn't experienced the slap of her palm, the rake of her nails, the sharpness of her teeth or the hardness of her brogue shoes.

They were all breathing heavily now; the girl most of all, while still making impotent efforts to break loose and backheel the shins of the dicks holding her.

Blunt's fingers tenderly caressed his smarting cheek. He said in a hard voice: 'Put her in a cell for an hour or two 'til she cools off.'

At his words, she made another violent effort to break free, kicked out wildly with brogue shoes, flared at Blunt angrily. 'Don't you dare put me in a cell! I'll strip that cop's coat off your shoulders. I'll have you back pounding the pavements. I'll raise a storm that'll repercuss right through to Washington.'

'Treat her as gently as possible,' instructed Blunt wearily. 'Now get her out of here before I get mad.'

She didn't go quietly. She resisted every inch of the way, so finally they had to lift her bodily, try to restrain her violently kicking feet as they carried her from the sweat room.

That just left me and Blunt.

Slowly, thoughtfully, he took off his bowler hat, mopped his forehead with a large white handkerchief and then wiped the sweat off his hat-band.

'I kinda get the feeling you didn't handle her the right way,' I told him.

His blue eyes stared at me angrily. Without thinking, his fingers once again tenderly massaged his smarting cheek. I could see the red imprint of her fingers like they'd branded on him. Slight and feminine she might have been, but she certainly packed a wallop.

Blunt growled despairingly. 'How can you handle a dame like that? She's uncooperative, wilful, over-imaginative and unmanageable.'

'Women are like horses,' I told him gently. 'They have to be broken in. Some can be handled easily, quickly become meek and docile. Others are tough and wilder and need an expert to tame them.'

'I'm policing a city, not staging a rodeo,' he said drily.

I took a cigarette pack from my pocket, offered him one, lit up myself. 'I'm not doing anything special right now,' I said offhandedly.

He came right over, right up close, chest touching mine, blue eyes staring into mine. 'No you don't, Janson,' he said grimly.

I tried to look innocent. 'Don't what?'

'Keep away from that dame,' he warned. 'She's trouble.

Trouble all the way. She's the kinda dame who'll do what she says, contact Washington and try and turn this department inside out. So far, neither me or my men have stepped out of line with her. And I don't intend they shall, Janson. So if you've got any crazy notions about going down to that cell and having a heart-to-heart talk with her, you can wipe it right off your slate.'

'Maybe *I* could make her a reasonable approach,' I said slyly-

He flushed. 'Nothing doing, Janson,' he snarled. 'Nothing doing.'

I shrugged good-naturedly. 'Okay,' I said. 'Have it your way. Now, how about something for the press? What's behind this explosion?'

He frowned angrily, bit his lip. 'The girl's the key to everything, Janson,' he said. 'Stinks department analysed every bit of dust, ballistics have scrutinized every piece of metal. The story's clear enough. A booby-trap parcel sent through the post to that dame. The commissionaire accepted the parcel in her absence, took it up to her apartment and left it on the table. One hour later ...!'

'You don't really think the dame sent it to herself?'

'Have sense, Janson,' he rasped. 'Does she look nuts?'

'Maybe she resented you suggesting she was crazy.'

He took a deep breath. 'Look at it from my angle, Hank. We've got nothing on the dame, nothing on anyone. But another bomb like that might kill lots of folk. I've just gotta move all hell to trace the sender. The dame's the key. Somebody she *knows* sent her that parcel.'

'Maybe she doesn't know them,' I put in. 'Maybe somebody was employed to send it.'

'She must have an inkling of why it was sent,' he snapped irritably. 'Somewhere, somehow there's a connecting link between her and the guy responsible.'

'Why don't you ask her nice and reasonable like,' I said gently.

'Look, Janson,' he said, hands working at his sides. 'Why

don't you go away now, nice and reasonable like. Otherwise ...'

'Otherwise what?'

'Otherwise I might be tempted to ease your exit with the toe of my boot.'

'Cut it out,' I grinned. 'Today isn't the end of the world. Don't let a spitfire knock you off balance.'

Slowly, reluctantly, he grinned back. 'Woudn't you like to take her across your knee, Hank? Tan the life out of her.'

'Well,' I said thoughtfully. 'I'd certainly like to take her across my knee. And what would be much more interesting ...'

'Okay, okay,' he interrupted quickly. 'I can use my imagination too.'

'What *are* you gonna do about her?'

He took a deep breath. 'I don't know. Hold her for a coupla hours until she's simmered down. Try questioning her some more. There's nothing else I can do. She's legally clean, no good reason I should hold her. If she won't answer questions, I can't make her. I can't prove she's withholding information.'

I said thoughtfully: 'She seems a determined kinda dame. If I were you, I'd quit worrying about the bomb and start worrying about your job. She acts like a dame who has got influence in the right places.'

'Any time anyone wants my job, they can have it,' snarled Blunt. 'Any time anyone thinks it's fun trying to keep a City clean, visiting the morgue to see the procession of stiffs that arrive and daily wading knee-deep in the sordid, corrupted lives of perverted killers, and criminals, he's ...'

'Any time you wanna quit,' I told him, 'I'll speak to the Chief, find you a niche in the *Chronicle* writing a daily feature.'

'There's only one reason I don't quit, Hank,' he said seriously. 'There's no end to all this. There's room for a dozen more of my rank with treble the man-power. It's a never-ending battle, cleaning up the vice, studying every crime that's committed and tracking down the criminals. Doing all that doesn't give us time for our real work.'

'What's your real work?'

'Crime prevention,' he said. 'The improvement of city

living so that crimes never get committed.'

'Maybe it's a good thing you haven't time to get around to crime prevention.'

He looked at me sharply. 'Why's that?'

'Then it would be me out of a job,' I grinned.

3

It was three hours before they let her loose. From the bar across the road I saw a coupla uniformed cops escort her through the swing doors, saw her quit them with a toss of her head and march proudly and arrogantly down the steps to the pavement, where she glanced both ways for a taxi.

I tossed a dollar bill on the counter, dived across the road in front of chromium-plated bonnets and raised my fedora to her like I was a gentleman. 'Excuse me, ma'am,' I said, politely.

She stared at me like I was something even the road sweeper avoided.

'You don't remember me?' I said gently.

'I certainly do not!' she said haughtily.

The dame had a private and personal iron curtain built around her that beat anything the Russians had thought up. It needed psychology to penetrate it.

'I saw you getting pushed around by them dumb cops,' I told her.

The iron curtain began to melt. 'You saw them?' she said excitedly. 'You saw the way they were treating me?'

'I was in the sweat room,' I told her. 'I saw everything that happened. It was crazy the way they kept asking you the same questions over and over again.'

'You're just the man I wanna meet,' she said eagerly. 'You were an actual eye-witness? You saw the way I was pushed around, saw the way I was ill-treated?'

I side-stepped her question deftly. 'I saw everything that happened.' I assured her.

Her face was flushed with excitement, her eyes gleaming purposefully. She took me by the arm like I was a valuable prize she was afraid to lose, said urgently: 'Where can we talk?'

Then the excitement drained out of her abruptly, a kinda veil came down over her eyes. 'Wait a minute,' she said suspiciously. 'What do you know about it anyway? What were you doing there?'

She was the kinda dame who wouldn't believe she had ten toes, unless seven independent accountants swore a solemn oath and put it in writing. I plunged my hand in my pocket, pulled out my press card. 'Reporter,' I explained. 'It's my job nosing around.'

She examined the press card with care, then stared into my face shrewdly. 'You could make a real song and dance about what they did to me,' she said.

'Could do,' I agreed.

'Listen,' she said with sudden resolution. 'Let's take taxi to my apartment. We can talk there in comfort.' I flagged a passing taxi, opened the door for her and then remembered about the bomb.

'Excuse me, lady,' I said. 'You sure you wouldn't prefer my club?'

'My apartment will be okay,' she said coolly and leaned forward, gave an address to the driver through the speaking tube. It wasn't the address where the explosion had taken place. I settled down comfortably on the seat beside her, noticed her windjammer was still open and cleared my throat noisily. 'You lived long on West Side?'

'Four weeks,' she said tersely. 'Chicago's new to me. I come from Ohio,'

I eyed her blue jeans, her dishevelled hair and those canary yellow socks. It wasn't the kinda get-up dames on West Side usually wore. Or ever wore, come to that. I plunged. 'Listen,' I said. 'Maybe I'm a little slow. But I heard your apartment got spattered around, mixed up a little with a trick postal packet. Where are we going now? Another apartment?'

Her eyes narrowed dangerously. 'Are you cross-examining me?'

I held up my hands pacifically. 'Wouldn't dream of it. Never entered my mind. I just wondered ... how ...?'

'I booked another apartment by phone at police head-quarters,' she told me abruptly. 'I've got to live somewhere, haven't I? Any objections?'

I gulped. 'No,' I said. 'But it did seem rather strange, and ...'

'Listen, Bighead,' she snapped. 'If you're on the level and wanna help me get back at them cops for the way they treated me, just string along. But if you're playing some line of your own, wanna pump me for information, you'd better quit now or you'll find I'm a dangerous dame to push around.'

I was sweating. I eased my finger around my collar band. 'I'm just a friendly kinda guy,' I told her meekly. 'I'm not looking for trouble of any kind.'

She scrutinized me carefully, made no secret she was weighing me up. Finally she said, doubtfully: 'Stick around anyway. It won't take long to find out what kinda guy you really are.'

When the taxi pulled up outside the apartment block. I opened the door for her. She sailed out like a queen, regally mounted the steps, whisked through the swing doors with a majestic air, not even giving me another glance, taking it for granted I would pay the taxi-driver and trail in behind her like a trained spaniel.

It was a swell joint, more like a hotel that rented apart-ments instead of single rooms. The carpet in the entrance hall was a rich, deep wine colour; plush-covered, comfortable armchairs were scattered around for the convenience of visitors, and at the far end of the entrance hall a uniformed commissionaire was opening a door for the dame, a door marked *'Office.'*

I didn't wanna miss a thing. The commissionaire had the

door half-closed behind her by the time I got there. I gave him a haughty nod, widened the door and strode in after her.

It wasn't an office, it was an emporium. The carpet was so thick it felt like I was sinking into it, and the guy behind the huge oak desk, who was obviously the apartment manager, was dressed like a Fifth Avenue tailor's advertisement. He was standing up for Miss Pinder, smart and immaculate, tall and impressive, and his face exhibiting the usual phoney, polite smile of welcome that was indispensable to his trade.

'Good afternoon, Miss Pinder,' he said suavely, but already the smile was becoming frozen and his manner distant as his eyes swiftly appraised her.

You couldn't really blame the guy. Those apartments had to be expensive, and he was accustomed to dealing with folk from the high income group. Miss Pinder didn't look like one of them. She looked like she might have arrived in town that day, having hitchhiked in dusty lorries.

He said in a faintly disbelieving voice: 'I understand you wish to rent an apartment?'

'You're the guy I spoke to on the 'phone, aren't you?' she rapped.

'Why …yes, I imagine so,' he said reluctantly.

'I told you what I wanted,' she said sharply. 'Lounge bedroom and study; bathroom and kitchen; all furnished.'

'That's right, Miss Pinder,' he said doubtfully. 'I have it prepared.'

'Good,' she said. 'Did you get in the liquor I ordered, have it installed.'

'Why … er … yes, Miss Pinder.' He was transferring his weight from one foot to the other like he was standing on red-hot coals. You could almost read his thoughts. He didn't figure she was worth a dime. But on the other hand, he'd gauged accurately her firebrand nature and didn't want to touch off her anger.

'Okay,' she said. 'Snap it up. Give me the key.'

'I … er … the keys!' He made a pretence of going through the drawers, knowing full well where they were but wanting to play for time. At last he found the key in the centre drawer. He didn't pass it across the desk, instead he put it on the desk in front of him. 'Excuse me, Miss Pinder,' he said apprehensively. 'There's just one or two little formalities to be undertaken.'

'Sure, sure, sure,' she said disinterestedly. 'Papers and things to sign. Usual routine. Shoot me the works, I'll put my cross on them.'

He fumbled in another drawer, pulled out more papers. Completely self-composed, she pushed a paper-weight and a chromium-plated inkwell to one side, edged one haunch onto the edge of his desk and impudently half-sat there, swinging one foot while she watched him impatiently.

He was nervous now, sweating slightly. 'If you'll just fill in here ...' he indicated with his forefinger.

She dug down in her handbag, couldn't find what she was looking for, impatiently up-ended it on the desk. A bewildering assortment of odds and ends rolled over the beautifully polished oak desk: three or four worn lipstick tubes, a powder compact, a man's wallet, a gold cigarette case, a nickel-plated lighter, a comb, a coupla boxes of matches and, of all the crazy things for a dame to carry around, two spark plugs!

The manager stared, gulped. I saw his lower lip trembling with emotion. But if the dame sensed his perturbation, she certainly showed no signs of it. Somewhere among that odd collection scattered on that table, she discovered her fountain pen, hastily and impatiently began to fill in the form.

The manager watched her doubtfully, licked his lips nervously, raised his eyes to mine and then looked away again quickly, almost guiltily. She stopped writing, stared at the form, was reading it while automatically she fumbled a cigarette from her case, lit it with a match and tossed the dead stalk on to the desk top.

The manager watched every move she made with undisguised anguish. His eyes followed the flight of the match through the air, a shudder shook him as it landed on his hitherto spotlessly clean desk, and he was fighting to keep distaste from screwing up his lips as he reached out, picked up the match between finger and thumb like a dead rat and carefully dropped it into the large, chromium-plated ashtray on the floor beside his desk.

She smoked like a man. Without removing the cigarette from her mouth, she said. 'Can't *you* fill in all this nonsense about security number and so on?' The cigarette bobbed between her lips as she spoke.

The manager gulped, and his eyes were suddenly gleaming with inspiration. His job was to make sure he got clients able to pay the high rents required. He saw a heaven-sent opportunity to assure himself on this point without offending a possible genuine client.

'Of course, if you haven't your security number you can always give your bank as a reference,' he said glibly.

She kinda froze, stared at the form without moving for several seconds. Then she slowly raised her head, stared straight at him.

There was a sickly grin on his face. 'If that happens to suit you, of course, Miss Pinder,' he said nervously.

'What's biting you?' she rasped. 'Worried about your dough?'

He was. The last thing he wanted to say was that he wasn't. But he hadn't the nerve to say he was. 'Why ... er ... we have certain formalities ...'

Contemptuously she picked up her wallet, opened it up. Even my eyes musta bulged. It was crammed with currency. Not piddling five and ten spots, not even good clean honest century notes. No, this was real dough. Grand notes, maybe thirty or forty of them, stuffed carelessly into that wallet, carried around casually in a scruffy-looking handbag. Yet far more impressive than anything was the casual way she peeled off five of those notes from her wad, leisurely tossed them across the desk at the manager. 'Tuck those under your belt, Shylock,' she sneered. 'Let me know when you want some more.'

He picked up the notes slowly, hardly crediting his eyes as he shuffled them into an even wad. 'Of course, this wasn't necessary, Miss Pinder,' he said with an oily smile. 'We render a monthly statement, and it's not necessary for our clients to pay in advance.'

She ignored him, slipped down off the desk, scooped her possessions together with two hands, shovelled them into her handbag. 'Do I get that key or don't I?' she snarled.

'Of course, of course.' he said promptly, almost falling over himself to be polite now, his greasy smile working to perfection.

She took the key, turned around, said to me bitterly. 'Don't you despise these kinda folk? When they look at anyone, all they see between their ears is a dollar sign. If there aren't enough 0s following it, they crinkle their nose. If there is enough 0s following it, they treat you like royalty.'

The manager had beaten us to the door, was opening it, standing there smiling greasily, almost half-bowing us out.

'You slimy jerk,' she said contemptuously as we passed through.

He nodded, smiled like she was saying pleasant things about him.

'How does a guy get that way?' she asked me. 'That's not a man. That's a dressed-up monkey. His type makes me sick to my belly.'

'Some day, some time, someone's gonna take you on their knee and tell you about the big, Almighty American dollar,' I told her. 'The all-powerful symbol that controls the world and human nature.'

'Don't get philosophical with me,' she cut in coldly. The commissionaire, having caught the manager's eye, was smiling at us, bowing us over to the elevator. As we walked towards it, she commented: 'Only folk who haven't got dough think it's worth something.'

'Sounds like a problem Socrates once pondered about,' I mused. 'Socrates asked himself: 'What's it better to be, a simple man content with his simple way of life, contented like a hog content with its hog-wash, or on the other hand, a wise man, full of wisdom and knowledge but bowed down by worry because of all that he knows and understands.'

'Don't go intelligent on me,' she snapped. 'Let's go get that drink, Bighead!'

4

It was a swell apartment. Any businessman bringing his wife to Chicago for a month who could afford the dough this furnished apartment cost wouldn't have had a thing to complain about. Neither would his wife.

She glanced around the lounge critically, nodded with approval when she saw the cocktail bar had been well stocked. Three rooms led off the lounge. One to the black-and-white tiled kitchen, one to the study with its streamlined, gleaming chrome and glass-topped desk and ivory-white telephone.

The third room was the bedroom. I trailed along behind her on this tour of inspection, particularly noticed how the bed, with its beautifully laundered, pink lacework counterpane and frilly bedside lamp, seemed so feminine and dainty, such a contrast to her in dusty, ill-fitting jeans and windjammer.

She tested the bed with her hand, pressed down on it and nodded her head approvingly. She sat on it, bounced up and down. 'Not bad,' she said approvingly. 'Try it.'

I sat on the bed beside her, bounced myself up and down a coupla times. My shoulder brushed against hers, and in the same moment we realized we were sitting there like a coupla seventeen-year-olds. Maybe she realized more. I certainly did. She was an attractive dame, I was a virile member of the opposite sex and this was a bedroom!

She got up quickly, walked over and opened up the bathroom door, inspected the glistening array of bathtaps and enamel-ware. I wasn't sure, but I thought I detected just the slightest flush on her cheeks.

'You oughta be comfortable here,' I said.

'I can rough it,' she said. 'I can be comfortable almost anywhere.'

'The bed's mighty comfortable,' I pointed out.

This time there was no doubt about it. There definitely was a shy flush on her cheek. She turned abruptly, walked through to the lounge. 'What about pouring drinks, Bighead?' she called over her shoulder. 'That's what you came up for.'

She sure got service in that joint. There were even fresh ice-cubes in the ice-box. I mixed two Tom Collins, long drinks in cool glasses, the ice tinkling merrily as I twirled the glasses in my hands.

She sipped her drink, said with an almost surprised note in her voice: 'You musta mixed these before.'

'I've had a little practice.' I toasted her silently, stared deep into her hazel eyes and wondered what made her bluey-black hair so gleamingly silky.

She tore her eyes away. 'About those cops,' she said deliberately. 'What I suggest is we go see my lawyer, give him the full facts. He'll start an action for false imprisonment and indecent assault, and ask substantial damages. Meanwhile you can give it thick headlines, spread your own eye-witness story on the front page and give me say a quarter of the front page for my version of what happened.' She took a sip of her drink. 'You'll write my story for me, of course, but it'll have my name on it.'

'What about Washington?' I said drily. 'We oughta. take this as high as we can.'

'I'll handle that,' she said, in a matter-of-fact voice. 'I'll put a long-distance call through to Senator Jacobs, get the whole affair made the subject of a public enquiry.'

I finished my drink. I said slowly: 'You don't maybe figure you're getting a little out of line on this?'

She stared at me, eyes hard and one eyebrow arched enquiringly. I liked the way she lifted her eyebrow. Somehow it made the atmosphere warm and cosy. But her voice was hard ice-chips. 'What exactly does that mean?'

'It's like this,' I said tactfully. 'I try to be a reasonable kind of guy.'

As I spoke, her face was slowly changing, a dark frown puckering her forehead.

'Sometimes one can get a lopsided view of any trouble one's involved in. Now I'm only an observer. I've got no interest in this quarrel one way or the other. But from where I sit, it looks to me like you've got no real kick against the cops. Maybe they did stick you in the cooler for a coupla hours. But that was only to gain time to lick their wounds. The cops were merely doing their job. They were trying to protect the public, and they were trying to protect you as well. After all, somebody must be gunning for you if ...'

She banged her glass on the cocktail bar, stalked across the room with long, determined strides, opened the door and pointed: 'Out,' she said tersely.

I put down my glass slowly, reached for my fedora, put it on the back of my head and shrugged my shoulders. 'Looks like I was wrong.' I told her. 'I figured you had enough savvy to think for yourself. Looks like I was dead wrong and you've got a one-track mind.'

'Out.' she repeated tersely.

I walked towards the door, hesitated, dug down in my wallet: 'Could be you're in real trouble, lady,' I told her. 'Somebody's gunning for you. You never know, I may be able to help you sometime. Here's my card.'

'I don't want your card. I don't wanna see you again. Get out,' she snarled.

I shrugged, dropped my card on the cocktail cabinet, sauntered out past her into the corridor. I was tensed all the time. Those hazel eyes were flaming with anger, the soft curve of her jaw was set in a hard line. 1 half expected her heavy brogue to start swinging and speed my departure.

Instead, the door nearly separated from its hinges as she slammed it behind me, the crash of it echoing from wall to wall to the end corridor.

I shrugged my shoulders, fumbled myself a cigarette, lit it and set off towards the elevator.

'What a dame,' I told myself. 'What a dame!'

5

It was a clear day, with a blue sky in which the sun hung like a blinding, golden ball. Yet there was a cold nip in the air, the tang of the frozen North borne on the gusty wind that came straight in across the flats.

It was good to get in off the tarmac, prop my elbows on the counter of the bar and stare with interest at the chart adorned with ink-drawn propellers that certified this was the Deadwood Flying Club, licensed to sell wines and spirits to members and guests.

The bartender said: 'You ain't a member, are you, chum?'

'I'm invited by a member.'

'What name?' He wasn't looking at me now but instead was referring to a small, black-bound ledger.

'Miss Pinder,' I said. 'Miss Beryl Pinder.'

'Yeah, that's right,' he agreed. 'Name of Janson? I'll get you a drink. She'll be along later. What'll you take?'

'Rye.'

It was a small bar, but comfortable. At the end of the bar, three young fellas wearing windjammers were playing darts. Seated at the tables and talking of wind velocities, diving speeds and navigational problems were weirdly-dressed guys who seemed to have the humour and good spirits of children.

At the far end of the counter stood a uniformed pilot-officer, together with another officer in a different type of uniform. It was difficult to decide which looked the strangest.

The British flying-officer with his black, drooping, handlebar moustache making him look like a long-tusked, intelligent seal, or the American pilot, whose cropped, crew-cut hair and lean face made him resemble an inmate of Belsen.

The British pilot said: 'These jets are wizard, what? I mean ter say, you gain altitude like billy-o. But then, of course, old man, you lose the personal touch. What! It makes you just a jolly old automatic pilot. I mean, you're not *actually* flying yourself, merely handling the plane. It's too awfully fast to dive down and prang a chappie whose taking a pot at you with, I mean. What!'

'You've gotta modernize, though,' said Crew-cut. 'You've gotta keep on top, maintain and increase industrial output, absorb every new technical improvement, keep right bang up to date. I guess I feel just the same way as you about handling a Mustang. You kinda get the feel of it, like you're forking a bronco. You become part of it, glued to it, grafted to your ship so it's not your hands obeying your brain but the whole plane. Sure, that's when you get a kick out of flying. Now with these jets you ...' He broke off, looked out towards the tarmac.

One side of the club-house was entirely of glass, giving clear, uninterrupted view of incoming and departing planes. Crew-cut said urgently: 'This you've gotta see, brother. This you can't miss.'

He was steering the British pilot across to the window and, as though at a signal, the other Club members were drifting over to the window with interest gleaming in their eyes.

I was lonely sitting at the counter by myself. I got up, drifted over to the window, stared alongside the others.

Crew-cut musta had exceptionally sharp hearing. I could only just now hear it myself. The low hum of the small plane that was already in sight, a tiny dot in blue sky.

There was a tense silence and everyone was listening and watching, kinda half-leaning forward, expectant and apprehensive.

I didn't know what to expect, so I watched carefully. The plane grew rapidly bigger, a silver glitter as the sun flashed against its aluminium body. It was coming in now, coming in low and fast. We had a clear, uninterrupted view, and that small, flashing plane looked like a silver bullet as it headed in towards the airfield at a sharp angle.

I watched, felt my mouth go dry. There was something wrong, something terribly wrong. That plane was coming in to land. But it was coming in far too fast, and the angle of approach was far too sharp.

There was a strained tenseness in the atmosphere that had me in its grip too. I stared, heard my heart pounding loudly and painfully as I realized the pilot had miscalculated badly. It was plummeting down now, the roar of the engine echoing like the chatter of machine-gun fire, the thin scream of the wings cutting the wind, sounding like the distant wail of a one-note siren.

There were seconds to go before that plane spattered itself on the runway not a coupla hundred yards from us. I tensed, felt my limbs paralysed with shock, powerless to do anything to avert the tragedy. I wanted to turn my head, look away. But the paralysis had gripped all of me, so that unwillingly I stared as though hypnotised, watched that silver streak flash to destruction.

Only it didn't.

If I hadn't seen it happen, I'd never have believed it possible. That pilot musta had the gods on his side. At the last moment, the very last moment, the nose of the ship turned upwards. It was a smooth, upward turn, but executed so sharply my tortured brain expected to hear the wrench and tear of metal as the sudden, wrenching strain broke the plane's back.

Miraculously, the plane didn't snap in two, and before my disbelieving eyes, it zoomed upwards, almost standing on its tail, climbing, climbing, climbing, until it was but a tiny speck high above us. And it was in that moment I realized something that caused me to sweat.

The wheels of that plane hadn't been lowered! That pilot had had no intention of landing!

'See what I mean,' said Crew-cut.

'The fella's crazy,' said the British pilot admiringly. 'I mean to say, that's a devilish silly thing to do. The silly chappy nearly buried himself to the back axles.'

'Yep,' agreed Crew-cut tensely. 'Watch this time.'

That plane had turned, was plummeting down again, glinting in the sun. The approach was from a different direction this time, across the runway and heading straight towards the Flying Club.

It's incredible how quickly a plane flying towards you can be on top of you. The roar of the engine was deafening, the shriek of the wind over the wings terrifying. That plane was coming straight at us, blasting straight at the Club window, expanding rapidly, as it hurtled straight towards us with wing-rending velocity.

We were all men in that Flying Club, yet there wasn't one of us who didn't instinctively recoil, crouch low and throw up a protective arm.

I saw the nose of that plane smashing at me like a battering ram, the wings spread wide and enveloping the horizon. Then it was the belly of the plane facing me, slipping upwards beyond my range of vision, there one moment, gone the next, leaving only the deafening roar of the engines in my ears.

There was a chorus of angry, startled and frightened exclamations. The frightened tension eased as angry words became the safety valve for the suppressed shock.

Crew-cut took out his handkerchief, mopped his forehead. 'The closest shave I've ever had,' he said.

The British pilot said: 'The old boy must be mad. Raving mad.' Then he added in a respectful voice: 'Skilful pilot. What! I mean, awful nerve and so on, but the dashed fellow certainly knows his stuff.'

Crew-cut gave him a strange, quizzical glance. 'Stick around, Bud,' he advised. 'Stick around. You'll meet the pilot.'

The plane was coming back again, this time approaching from the wrong end with the wind behind it. The wheels were lowered now, and that made the crazy dive even more spectacular.

I winced as, for the third time, it seemed that nothing could save the plane. It was driving in at a speed and an angle that guaranteed it would bury itself completely in the hard concrete. Then, miraculously, at the last moment the nose jerked upwards, the plane executed that incredible back-breaking vee-shaped upward turn, and this time the pilot came so close to the ground the wheels actually touched!

In the brief instants before the plane zoomed upwards out of sight, I saw the landing wheels spinning madly from their momentary contact with the runway.

'The old boy's absolutely crazy, of course,' said the British pilot. 'Abso-bally-lutely. But he's a whiz at handling a plane. Good job some of our lads aren't here. They'd be trying it too. They'd be just as crazy.'

We could still see the plane, exhibiting a series of acrobatics, looping the loop, zooming, spiralling, and the most difficult of all, the falling leaf.

The pilot was a nut. He was risking not only his own neck but the lives of other people. Yet even now, when he was looping and zooming, his plane glittering like a star, quite obviously indulging in an extreme and stupid piece of exhibitionism, I still had to admire the capable skill of the pilot.

A few minutes later, the plane came in, a beautiful landing this time, a perfect example of practised skill. The plane touched down on the runway, turned off and taxied towards the Club. The grease monkeys ran out to meet it, grasped it, guided it into position so it came to a standstill a few yards from where we were watching.

It was a small, two-seater plane with an open cockpit. I watched as the pilot pushed open the unbreakable glass cockpit canopy. I gulped, wiped the sweat from my brow.

Straightaway you could tell the pilot was a dame, because of the black hair peeping from beneath her flying helmet. The familiar windjammer, slacks and yellow socks would have been sufficient to identify her even if I hadn't been able to make out her features.

She jumped down from the plane, slim and athletic, lithe and attractive. She pulled off her flying helmet, so her silky hair was windswept, and strode towards the Flying Club with short, quick feminine steps, pulling off her fur-lined gloves at the same time.

You could have heard a pin drop. There were maybe a dozen men in there all watching her intently, breathless and silent.

It was incredible the effect she had upon them. A roomful of strong, virile men, and that slim figure, striding imperturbably towards the Club door, exerted over them a fascination that rendered them tongue-tied, awed and just a little nervous.

That wasn't the whole story. They were men, proud and self-conscious men, all flyers, and their pride had taken a eating. They knew plenty about flying, and they knew instinctively this slip of a dame could fly the pants off any of them. What made their medicine even more bitter and unpleasant to swallow was the fact she was a dame. Not a strong, virile male, but a slender little dame who shouda been leaning on their arm, staring up into their faces with adoration instead of striding self-confidently across the tarmac with a sureness of foot that showed she possessed nerves of steel.

There were a dozen pairs of eyes watching the club-room door as it swung open. She swept in completely self-possessed, threw them a casual, disinterested glance and walked straight to the bar.

'Make it a rye, Joe,' she said.

'Yeah, ma'am,' he said enthusiastically, and reached for a bottle.

I sauntered back to the bar, rested my elbows on the counter beside her. 'Remember me,' I said.

She glanced around, took my accepting her invitation for granted. 'Hiya, Bighead. Been waiting long?'

'Just long enough,' I told her.

'Set up another drink, Joe,' she ordered. 'Get me my

handbag, too.'

I extended my cigarette case. There were a dozen eyes watching in suspenseful silence as she took a cigarette, accepted my light and spoke with the cigarette bobbing up and down in her mouth.

'I asked you over on account I figured I acted pretty beastly the other day.'

It came straight from the shoulder. There were a dozen guys watching her intently, listening to every word she said. There's not a dame in a million will admit when she's in the wrong. She was the exception. She admitted it in public.

'You've had two or three nights to sleep on it,' I said. 'Time usually produces a more reasonable attitude.'

She stared at me, narrowed one eye. 'Don't get me wrong,' she snapped. 'I've got an angle. I was too hasty about letting you out of my sight. You're a guy with influence. I need your help. Someone's gotta put those cops in their place.'

Joe came up with my drink, handed the battered handbag over the counter to the dame. She opened it up, dug down for a grubby powder compact, dabbed at her face, used her lipstick with the disconcern of a girl in the seclusion of her bedroom sitting before her dressing table. Not by the flicker of an eye or a single glance did she show she knew she was the target for a dozen pairs of admiring but resentful masculine eyes.

'Don't expect too much of me,' I said. 'The *Chronicle* prints facts, not opinions.'

She arched her lips, held everyone in watchful suspense as she shaped them with the lipstick. She leaned forward, inspected her handiwork closely in the cracked mirror of the battered compact, snapped it shut, thrust it back into her handbag.

'Have another drink, then come to town with me,' she said. 'I've got something to show you.'

'That's a deal,' I told her. I caught Joe's eye, ordered the same again. Then, as he tilted the bottle, I became conscious of someone standing beside us. I glanced up just as he spoke.

'Hello old girl,' he enthused. 'Just simply must say how jolly wizard it was, the way you flew that kite. I mean, it was simply terrific. None of our chaps could handle a kite that way, if you see what I mean. What!' He was like a playful terrier, doggily friendly. If he'd owned a tail, it would have been wagging furiously.

She looked up at him with complete self-possession, looked him over carefully, allowed her cigarette smoke to blow in his eyes without appearing to do it intentionally.

'Say, you're English, aren't you,' she drawled.

He smiled – simpered is maybe a better word. 'Jolly old England. Like me to tell you about it? What! You know, dinner, a bottle of champagne and all that stuff?'

'Tell me,' she said seriously, 'do your girlfriends use that horse hair under your nose to swing on, or do you use it to frighten the enemy?'

He went red. I've never seen a guy go so red. 'I say, old thing,' he protested falteringly. 'I mean, it's not done to criticise. What. I mean, all the chaps have these things, you know.'

She drawled cuttingly: 'Shuddup and scram will you? I don't make dates. You're wasting your time. Get your shoulder under that hank of bull's wool and hump it some-where else.'

Crew-cut sidled alongside the reddened and sweating British pilot. He took up the cudgels on his friend's behalf. 'Justa minute, lady,' he drawled ominously. 'This guy's a visitor. It ain't polite to make cracks about his whiskers. It ain't polite to make cracks about visitors at all, especially guys who are friendly and don't wanna cause offence. Now watch you speak to the guy nice and polite like, without trying to show him how damned smart you are.'

Her eyes glinted dangerously. Her voice was pregnant with fury and indignation. 'How dare you speak to me that way,' she gasped.

The other guys were closing in now, forming a semicircle around her, which rapidly diminished in size. It was as though they'd been waiting for this, waiting for someone to revenge the smart of their bruised masculine pride. Crew-cut said: 'Apologize to the man. You can't talk to him that way.'

The British pilot, still red-faced, said pacifically: 'It's quite all right, really. Please excuse me, miss.'

But the other guys had crowded close now, prevented him from turning away. Crew-cut said in a loud, almost dominating voice: 'Apologise to the guy like I told you.'

She was breathing hard, the white bones of her knuckles gleaming as she clenched her fists tightly.

'Get away from me, all of you,' she spat at them. 'I didn't want anyone to talk to me. I told him where he got off, the same as I'm telling all of you.'

A guy with a tweed coat, baggy flannel trousers and a shock of black hair said, in a quiet, tense voice: 'This dame's needed cooling off for a long time. Maybe this is as good a time as any to dunk her in the cistern, show her she can't throw her weight around.'

There was an eager chorus of agreement, and almost instantaneously the mood changed from resentment to menace.

Maybe she'd been outta line in snubbing the British pilot quite so impolitely. But these guys were wanting to get back at her for no other reason than that she could fly the pants off them and had hurt their vanity. Almost without thinking, I found myself gliding between her and them. 'What say we have a drink all round,' I suggested cheerfully. I looked straight at the British pilot. 'You'll have a drink with the lady?'

She didn't give him a chance to reply. She pushed me angrily to one side, stood glaring around at them. 'Who's the first?' she challenged truculently. 'Who's gonna be the first to put a hand on me?'

She was only slight, but she possessed an inner courage that was almost frightening. The guy with the shock of black hair who'd spoken of dunking her discreetly allowed himself to be shouldered out of the way by the other fellas.

'Well!' she demanded, eyes flashing. 'Who's the first?'

The British officer, still red-faced, said: 'I apologize, miss. I should never have spoken to you without being introduced.'

Crew-cut said angrily: 'He's apologizing for nothing. You done him dirt, lady. You're a self-opinionated, cocky, vicious little bitch who ...'

I coulda warned him if there'd been time. But there wasn't. He reeled back, lips pursed up with the smart of his stinging cheek.

'The little wildcat!'

'Trades on being a woman!'

'Needs a good spanking.'

'Chuck it, old girl.' pleaded the British officer. 'Dash it, I mean, you just can't go around slapping chaps ...'

He learned she could. His face was not so red it couldn't get redder. The crack of her palm against his cheek was like the report of a pistol.

Maybe she'd have got away with it if only Crew-cut had been involved. But this was a British officer, a visitor in a strange land. It was the final insult that she could offer them and, as if at a signal, they moved in on her quickly.

'Now listen, fellas,' I protested quickly, and was immediately swept to one side. Then, as they grabbed her, some crazy streak of chivalry made me wade into them, try to wrest her loose.

It was hopeless, and I knew it even before I started. But I just couldn't help myself.

Three of them held me by the arms, and a fourth crooked his arm painfully around my neck.

'You gonna quit struggling, fella?' demanded one. 'Or do you wanna get the same?'

There was nothing more I could do for her, and I certainly didn't wanna get the same. I licked my bleeding lip. 'Okay,' I grunted breathlessly. 'I'll quit struggling.'

They didn't wanna miss anything. They kept a firm grip on me and trailed after the others. The dame wasn't enjoying it very much. Nobody enjoys being frog-marched. And as they dragged her across the tarmac towards the large water tank embedded in the ground, the white-overalled grease mechanics came running to watch, grinning all over their grease-smudged faces, gleeful at the prospects of seeing her dunked. All in all, it wasn't difficult to learn she wasn't a popular dame around that joint.

'Listen, fellas,' I pleaded. 'She's only a dame. Don't take it too hard.'

'Maybe he does want the same,' said one of them.

'Yeah, maybe he does.' They stared at me.

I licked my lips. 'All right,' I said. 'I'm not arguing.'

'Got more sense than she has.'

'Maybe she'll have more sense afterwards.'

They didn't push her in. They threw her in. They took her by arms and legs, swung forwards and backwards, let her go at the third swing so she rose spread-eagled into the air, fell flat like a jelly-fish dead in the centre of the tank. The water splashed everyone, and the displacement as she went under made the water flow and break against the concrete walls like breaking waves.

She was under only a coupla seconds. But it was a cold day and the water musta been almost freezing. She came up blowing like a whale, blinded by her soaked hair, her face already going blue.

The walls of the tank were high. She could only just reach up and curl her fingers over the edge. She tossed her head, got the hair out of her eyes, which were glowing redly like hot coals. Furiously, she tried to lift herself out, every line of her face expressing the anger she was gonna vent on them.

She hadn't the strength. She strained until her chin was level with her hands, clung for several seconds, found she couldn't make it and had to sink back into the water to get her breath.

Seven times she made the effort and seven times she had to sink back again, while her vanity-satisfied persecutors stood around laughing and jeering at her.

She wasn't ever gonna get out of that tank without help. The cold was slowly getting her, numbing her to the bone. Her strength was failing, her determination getting weaker and weaker. Anger had long ago died from her eyes, and now she was woebegone and pathetic, a half-drowned dame looking like a half-drowned rat, and on the point of crying with cold and misery.

'Listen, fellas,' I pleaded. 'She's had enough. Don't take it too far.'

Maybe even they were touched by her pathetic eyes and chattering teeth. They let me go so I could lean over the tank, get my hands beneath her armpits and try to lift her out.

She was slippery, she was heavy and I could feel her shivering violently. It took all my strength to lift her, pull her over the edge, drag her from the tank so that she could sprawl on the grass, chest heaving, teeth chattering.

Strangely enough, there were only the two of us there now. The rest of them had drifted away quickly, unwilling to face her when she recovered her strength.

'It isn't smart sitting around in wet things,' I told her. 'You'd better change somewhere, get dried off.'

She extended her hand to me and, as I hoisted her to her feet, she said through chattering teeth: 'Get me outta here, will ya? Get me outta here.'

'You'd better dry off,' I said. 'Borrow a suit of dungarees from someone.'

Her face was blue with the cold, her long, delicate fingers were white, bloodless and cramped. 'There's no place here,' she said. 'Just get me out of here, will ya? Take me home.'

'There's the club-room.'

'For heaven's sake,' she half-screamed. 'Take me home, will you?'

I got it then. As well as being half-frozen with cold, she was thoroughly humiliated. The sting of humiliation was the greater hurt. She couldn't bear to be around where those guys could see her, snigger at her.

'This way,' I grunted, took her by the arm and steered her across the tarmac to where my car was parked.

She'd lost all her athletic, self-assured confidence. She

stumbled, shivered, hung her head so her dripping black hair fell over her shamed face. From the corner of my eye, I watched those guys standing at a safe distance, watching speculatively and savouring every minute of her humiliation.

'Those swines,' she said ,through chattering teeth. 'I'll get even with them. Just wait until I get one of them on his own.'

I opened the door of my car for her, suppressed a sigh as she settled on the new upholstery, soaking it, a large puddle of water already forming between her feet.

I went around the other side, climbed in behind the driving wheel and made a racing start. If she didn't get out of those clothes soon, she stood a good chance of catching pneumonia.

She hunched beside me, teeth chattering like castanets, face mauve, and her black hair straggled across her cheek.

'Try the glove compartment,' I told her. 'I keep a brandy flask there.'

She sipped at it gratefully, shivering all the time. 'Step on it, will ya,' she snarled. 'I'm frozen stiff.'

I got her back to that swell apartment block, trailed behind her as she almost ran through the carpeted entrance lounge to the elevator doors. The commissionaire stared like his eyes would pop out of his head, and the apartment manager, who'd just emerged from his office, ducked back again quickly like he didn't wanna see her. She'd been living at the joint only three days, but it looked like he'd been getting more than his share of the rough end of her tongue during that short time.

'Snap it up, Charlie.' she chattered to the commissionaire. She slapped her arms up and down to get warm, spattered him with moisture.

The commissionaire gulped, stared woodenly in front of him as he operated the elevator, opened it on the floor she occupied.

Only then did she discover she'd left her handbag on the counter of the bar and had to wait shivering and agonized with cold while he got the master key.

As soon as we were inside, she made a dive for the bedroom. I sauntered over to the cocktail cabinet, mixed myself a drink. A few moments later I heard the spurt of the shower, and knew she'd stripped, was warming up under the hot shower.

I was halfway through my second drink when I heard the shower turned off and her voice. 'Hey,' she yelled.

I crossed to the bedroom door, opened it, stood just outside. 'Want me?'

'Yeah. Come in.'

I put down my glass, squared my shoulders, sidled cautiously into the bedroom. The door of the bathroom was open and one bare arm protruded, holding her soaked jeans and sweater.

'You want something?'

'Yeah,' she said from behind the door. 'Take these things, will ya? I've wrung them out. Dry them in front of the electric fire.'

'Sure.'

I went back to the lounge, switched on the electric fire, draped the sweater, the jeans, and a coupla other interesting items in front of the fire. Then I went back to the bedroom, knocked discreetly before I entered.

The bathroom door was still half-open. 'Is that you?'

'Yeah. Anything you want? Anything I can get you? Change of clothes in the wardrobe or something?'

'Haven't any other clothes.' Her voice was breathless like she'd been towelling hard.

I said in a louder voice: 'Want I should get you a change of clothes?'

Her face peered around the door, together with the tip of one bare shoulder. Her hazel eyes glared belligerently. 'You deaf or something?' she demanded. 'I just told you. I haven't any other clothes.'

I said: 'Oh.'

I took a deep breath, looked around that swell, expensive apartment and said 'Oh' again.

'What's so strange about that?' she demanded. 'All my clothes were destroyed in my other apartment.'

'But lady, that was three days ago,' I protested.

'I've been busy, Bighead.'

'Maybe a sleeping suit?' I suggested weakly. There wasn't a doll I knew who with all the dough this dame owned wouldn't pass three-quarters of her conscious life spending it on clothes. This dame sure was different. For three days she'd been wearing that trouser outfit and hadn't even bothered to buy herself a sleeping suit.

'You make coffee?' she demanded.

'When my arm's twisted.'

'I'm twisting it right now,' she snapped. 'Get a move on, will ya? I want rum in mine!'

It was a novelty meeting up with a dame quite so domineering as this one. By the time I'd made the coffee, placed it on a low table, I could hear her moving about in her bedroom.

'Coffee's ready,' I shouted.

What I meant was, should I hand the coffee to her through the bedroom door.

'Just coming,' she answered. 'Just coming.'

She'd told me the score. The only clothes she possessed were those drying in front of the fire. I settled myself comfortably on the settee, lit a cigarette, stared at the bedroom door and waited expectantly.

'Okay,' she said as she came through. 'Start pouring, Bighead.'

6

I shoulda known an expensive apartment like that took care to cater for its clients' every comfort. Much to my disappointment, I realized the bathroom musta been well-stocked with towels.

One of them she'd draped around her waist like a skirt, and as it parted when she walked, I saw she'd draped a smaller towel round her loins like a napkin. A third towel was pulled tightly across her breasts and knotted at the back. But even through the thick towelling there was ample confirmation of the charms her tight-fitting sweater had revealed.

With complete lack of self-consciousness she settled herself at the other end of the settee, crossed her long slim legs. 'Cigarette,' she said.

Silently I gave her one, held a match for her, noticed the softness of her skin.

'Coffee,' she ordered.

'Black?'

'If it's good coffee.' Her tone was insultingly sceptical.

'Sugar?' I said, swallowing my annoyance.

'One spoonful.'

'Anything else you want me to do?' I said sarcastically.

As though my waiting on her was the most natural thing in the world, she said off-handedly: 'Yeah. Ginger snaps. There should be some in the kitchen.'

I didn't resent helping her. After all, for a dame, she'd just had pretty rough handling. But it was her superior, almost lordly attitude I resented. Just for a moment, hot, angry words trembled on my lips. Then again I remembered her blue face, chattering teeth and pathetically soaked and drooping figure.

I got the biscuits.

'While you're up you can get my brush and comb from the bedroom,' she told me.

I got the brush and comb. I was pleased to do it. It was the first naturally feminine desire she'd expressed.

And still she'd given me no explanation why she'd invited me to meet her at the Flying Club.

I sipped my coffee, nibbled a biscuit. 'Feel warmer now?' I asked politely, waiting for her to broach the main subject.

'How d'you expect me to feel after a hot shower? What are hot showers for?'

'Have you ever once spoken politely and quietly?' I countered. 'Do you ever speak to any one real sociable like?'

She gave me a sideways glance, her clear hazel eyes hostile and challenging.

'Are you suggesting there's something wrong with my attitude?'

That hot shower had warmed her temper as well as her body. Every word she said, every line of her beautiful face showed her low temper flashpoint needed only a spark to cause an explosion.

'I'm suggesting nothing,' I said cautiously. 'Merely making a statement.'

She sniffed daintily, somehow making it sound like a contemptuous snort. She sipped her coffee, moved her position on the settee. Those towels were securely knotted. My innermost hopes they would slip were doomed to disappointment. But she hadn't made a dressmaker's job of it, and the towelling skirt provided a fashion innovation I found wholly delightful.

She said icily: 'Do you have to keep staring at my legs?'

'I don't have to. But while I can choose, that's my preference.'

'You men are all the same,' she said bitterly.

'Shows you need educating. We're all very different.'

'What kick do you get out of it?' she asked contemptuously. 'Any dame in a swimming costume reveals far more than I am now.'

'You're overlooking one little point,' I said gently. 'There isn't any other dame in a swimming costume around. There's only you.' Even I was astonished how my words seemed to suggest we were alone together, close and intimate.

There were two red spots burning high up on her cheeks. 'Damn it. D'you have to keep staring that way?'

'Getting you worried?' I asked easily.

She lifted her hereafter from the cushion, strained the towelling skirt around her more tightly. It didn't cover any more of her, but it accentuated the softness of her curves.

I admired her with natural, masculine enthusiasm for soft curves.

Irritably she banged down the coffee cup, picked up her brush and comb and began to brush her hair furiously. Her cheeks were flushed and her eyes sparkled angrily.

Or was it anger?

She had good shoulders; gently rounded, warm, soft shoulders. I watched the soft, liquid play of the smooth flesh on her arms as she vigorously brushed hair back over her ears. Her skin was a kinda light, golden brown, but where her upraised arms revealed the hollows of her armpits, the skin was a creamy white, subtlety and intimately fascinating.

As though she suddenly felt her actions were a brazen display, she lowered her head, started vigorously brushing her long, black silky hair as it hung concealingly over her flushed face.

I transferred my gaze to the towelling skirt. The skin of her thigh was the same, light golden brown as her shoulders. Her vigorous arm movements vibrated her body. I knew if I were close enough she would smell sweet, clean and fresh, like rose petals.

Her hot eyes were watching me through the silken screen

of her hair. I sensed her stare before I raised my own eyes to hers.

She looked away quickly, thrust her hair back over her head, brushed her hair back away from her face. She said in a hard, strained voice, 'Damn you, stop staring, will you?'

'Maybe you've got a jigsaw puzzle around,' I suggested helpfully.

'Don't be funny,' she snapped. Her cheeks were still flushed, and now her hot eyes were soft and swimmy. 'Just don't keep staring like I'm the fat woman at a circus.'

'You don't look that way to me,' I said 'Shall I tell you the way you look to me? You look fascinating. Those shoulders now, so smooth and round. Your measurements too. I'd say you're just about right. Around the top, I'd say you'd measure about ...'

'Shuddup!' she almost screamed.

I grinned at her serenely. She glared back, flushed and breathing hard.

'Your hips too,' I went on gently. 'I'd say they were in perfect proportion, and you're leggy, long slim legs that ...'

Anger had made her so breathless and so flushed that her eyes were hot and sultry.

I was sitting at the other end of the settee, not a yard separating us. Yet her aim was bad, the hair brush whistling over my shoulder, smashing against the wall behind me.

I stared at her.

She glared back.

I licked my lips. There was anger smouldering inside me, and nervous reaction from shock. There'd been plenty of steam behind that brush. If it had caught my head or cheek I'd have needed stitches.

'You vicious, selfish little bitch,' I gritted. 'You crazy lunatic.' My voice trembled.

Her eyes showed she'd instantly regretted her mad impulse. 'I told you to stop staring,' she said defensively. 'You wouldn't stop staring!'

'Listen, wildcat,' I said with a steely note in my voice. 'You asked me to meet you at the Flying Club. You had something to tell me. Since then, you've been sitting there wriggling your half-naked body around in front of me. Am I supposed to be blind? Suppose you tell me what's on your mind so I can clear out of here quick.'

I was all worked up at the narrowness of my escape. Just figure it. One hasty, bad-tempered action and I mighta been staunching blood, might even have lost my eye.

She realised it too. The colour had drained from her cheeks, leaving her pale, and frail-looking. Her hazel eyes were tinged with apprehension. 'I didn't mean to throw it. I didn't know what I was doing. You just got me madder and madder, continually looking at me that way and ...'

'Skip the apologies,' I interrupted. 'What was on your mind when you asked me to meet you?' I got up from the settee, reached for my fedora.

'It's ... it's ... it's nothing to tell you, only something to show you.'

'Put it on show, sister,' I growled. 'Let's get it over before my throat gets cut.'

Her hazel eyes were worried, even a little reproachful. Mutely they expressed a regret for what she'd done. 'I can't show you here. It's downstairs. Downstairs in the garage.'

'Let's go then,' I said abruptly.

'But...' Her hazel eyes slipped from me to her clothing steaming in front of the electric fire.

'Yeah,' I said thoughtfully. I pulled at my lower lip, eyed her, eyed her drying clothes. 'Okay,' I sighed. I took off my fedora, skimmed it across to an occasional table, sat on the settee again with a grunt of impatience. 'I guess I can risk another ten minutes here.'

She was watching me cautiously, very quiet now, somehow subdued.

There was a long silence. She said quietly: 'Mr Janson?'

'Yeah,' I said, in a fed-up voice.

'I'm sorry for what just happened,' she choked. It sounded like it was being dragged out of her by wild horses, like it was the first time she'd ever apologized in her life. Maybe it was!

'Forget it,' I snarled. 'It didn't worry me a little bit.'

'It didn't?' Her voice was gently and incredulously disbelieving.

'Naw,' I grunted. 'Practically every day, a dame tries to pulp my face with a hairbrush. It proves how gentle and feminine they are.'

The colour was back in her cheeks, her eyes glinting. 'I've apologized,' she rasped. 'D'you want I should go on my knees?'

I looked at her knees.

She coloured furiously. 'You're doing it again,' she warned.

'Am I to blame?' I demanded. 'Most other dames I know usually wear a skirt.'

This time she turned beetroot colour. I flinched instinctively as she jumped to her feet. Then I relaxed as, with a toss of her head, she padded across the room to the telephone.

It was gonna be a long call. She pulled up her chair, sat down, rested her elbows on the table as she put the receiver to her ear.

I lounged back comfortably on the settee, watched her closely. Only her shoulders were on show now, but they were worth watching.

'Long distance,' she said.

When they answered, she gave them a New York number.

She drummed her fingers impatiently on the table while she waited. I finished my cigarette, stubbed it out in the ashtray.

'Gimme a cigarette,' she demanded over her shoulder.

I sauntered across to her, held a packet of cigarettes beneath her nose. She didn't look up, took a cigarette and placed it between her lips. I had to lean over to give her a light.

The soft skin of her bare shoulders was so warm it seemed to glow. Her hair was still damp, and curled tantalisingly at the nape of her neck. I couldn't resist it. I bent over and huffed hot breath on the back of her neck.

She shuddered deliciously.

I huffed again.

She made a half-turn towards me and checked herself as her number answered.

I huffed some more, watched her shuddering so deliciously as she talked into the 'phone.

'Put me through to Madame Gaynor.'

I did it differently this time, blew gently on her left shoulder, worked slowly across to her right shoulder. She shuddered just as deliciously, put her head on one side, pressed her ear against her hunched shoulder.

'This is Beryl Pinder,' she said in to the phone. 'Note my new address.'

I blew gently on the nape of her neck, ran slowly higher so that little damp curls rippled like wind blowing across a field of tall wheat. She hunched up her shoulder higher, arched her back, gave an involuntary shudder of pleasure.

'I want a complete new wardrobe,' she said into the phone. 'I want rigging out with everything.'

Gently I teased the fine hairs at the nape of her neck with my finger.

'Right away,' she said into the telephone. 'I haven't a thing to wear.'

My finger traced a subtle pattern from the nape of her neck up to and around her ear. She put her head on one side, wriggled one bare shoulder and still went on talking into the phone.

'That's no good. I want someone here right away. Catch the next plane over. I don't care if they have to work all night.'

I used the tip of my fingernail, drew it softly and quickly across her shoulder so it caused her to shudder.

'That's it,' she said into the telephone. 'Right away. Don't waste any time at all.'

She put down the receiver quickly, sat the way she was with head lowered, kinda waiting and expectant.

My forefinger traced a pattern across her shoulders, down the hollow of her back as far as to the knotted towel. She raised her head, arched backwards towards me.

I pressed my hot lips to the nape of her neck and, as I did so, heard her involuntary sob of emotion.

It was natural and simple the way my arms went around her, natural and simple the way her hands covered mine, pressed them against her. She was hot and trembly, heart beating quickly, her fingers strong and passionate as they clamped over mine.

'You've got beautiful shoulders,' I whispered.

There was a long silence. She said in a husky voice: 'Cut it out.'

'It's true,' I assured her. 'I'm not just inventing pleasant things to say.'

'I don't mean that,' she said hoarsely. 'I mean the other. Cut it out.' It obviously needed an effort, but she got determination into her voice.

'What's the trouble?' I whispered. 'Something annoying you?'

She didn't reply, breathed quickly.

'Something you don't like?' I asked insistently.

'You know what I mean.'

'What's bothering you? Something unpleasant.'

Silence except for her deep breathing; and she still wouldn't turn her head to look at me.

'Is *this* unpleasant,' I demanded insistently.

'You know it isn't,' she said huskily. 'But you've gotta cut it out.'

'If you like it, why stop it?'

It was a logical question and I suspected the answer. But I wanted to hear it from her own lips.

'It doesn't stop here, does it?' she whispered.

'D'you want it to?' My lips brushed the back of her neck and I felt her shudder with pleasure.

'Cut it out,' she pleaded breathlessly. 'Cut it out, will you?'

It takes two to make a bargain, and love-making is essentially a duet. Not even a fever specialist would have said I had a low temperature at that moment. But I like my companions to be as eager and as anxious as me.

'I'll cut it out,' I said. 'If you'll let me.'

She still clutched my hands firmly like she was never gonna let them go. She stayed that way for some time before I realized the way it was with her.

'Do something,' she whispered frantically. 'Break it up, will you?'

It was difficult to believe she was the dame who a few minutes earlier had nearly brained me. I'd wanted to force an admission from her that this was pleasant, but I'd got much more. She'd opened the floodgates of her emotions. She didn't only find it pleasant, she hadn't the strength or will-power to break it up! She was pleading with me to break it up.

And I had to be smart and show her what a big, tough, self-controlled guy I was. I broke it up, wrestled my hands away from her and sauntered back nonchalantly to the settee like I did this a dozen times a day.

I might have been fooling her, but I wasn't fooling myself. Another half-a-minute of holding her like that and I wouldn't have been able to pry myself away with an oyster opener.

I lit a cigarette, shot a glance at her. She was sitting in exactly the same position. At the telephone with her back towards me, sitting rigid like she was undergoing intense strain and was fighting to keep her emotions under control.

Maybe she was, at that!

I sat smoking while she sat that way for almost ten minutes, neither of us exchanging a word. Then, abruptly, quietly and with the self-possessed air of a hostess getting up from the tea table to bring hot water for the pot, she rose, came across to the fire.

'I think these are dry enough now,' she said quietly, and whisked her clothes away into the bedroom.

I listened to the fast beating of my heart and waited for it to slow down. But it didn't. Because that bedroom door was still half open, and my imagination was stimulated, working overtime.

I was still hot and desirous when she emerged from the bedroom a quarter of an hour later. But she cooled me quicker than she'd been cooled off in that water tank. It was as though by putting on jeans and the windjammer she completely cloaked all her femininity. And what guy can feel gooey about a dame who ain't feminine?

'Let's go, Bighead,' she said crisply. 'This is gonna interest you.' Her hazel eyes barely rested upon me, and her efficient, self-confident air sent my temperature dropping to my boots, despite the admitted tightness of that yellow sweater.

I grabbed my fedora, had to lengthen my strides to catch her at the door of the apartment.

'Basement,' she told the elevator hop crisply.

Many modern apartment blocks have their own garages in the basement. They're parking sites rather than repair depots. That's why there was only one attendant and one mechanic on duty as she strode quickly across to the solitary raised ramp upon which was a cream and white coupe.

She didn't hesitate, walked right under the jacked-up car, beckoned me and pointed. I ducked my head, followed the direction of her pointing finger.

Yeah, it was nasty to see. Brake couplings neatly sawn in two by a hacksaw.

7

I moved in close, examined the couplings carefully. They hadn't been cut right the way through. The tiny, uncut section had snapped under the pressure of applied brakes.

'When did it happen?' I demanded.

'Last night.'

'It was deliberate,' I said slowly.

There was a mocking smile on her lips. 'A regular Sherlock Holmes, aren't you?'

'Lucky you found out about it,' I said. 'Might have had a nasty crash.'

She arched one eyebrow, her eyes half-laughing, half mocking. 'Take a look at the left front wing,' she told me.

I ducked out from under the car, walked around front, and stared at the concertina'd wing. It was a good car, a valuable car. It was capable of exceedingly high speeds. I shuddered as I thought what would have happened if those brake couplings had snapped when her foot was well down on the throttle.

I went back to her. She was still under the ramp, examining the underneath of the car with an experienced and critical eye. The garage attendant and a lanky, gawky mechanic stood watching.

'Hey, you, give me a coupling spanner,' she ordered.

The gawky mechanic crossed to a nearby bench, came back with an assortment of spanners. She took one, began to use it as the mechanic stepped back, watched her owlishly, mouth open, lower jaw hanging.

'It was done deliberately,' I told her.

She'd got a smudge of oil on her cheek, was grunting as she strained on the spanner. 'Pull that light over,' she instructed.

I pulled the light around so she could see better. 'Someone's gunning for you,' I said.

She grunted as she strained a nut loose, quickly and skilfully unthreaded it with nimble fingers. 'Kinda looks that way, doesn't it,' she said disinterestedly.

'Is that what you wanted to show me?'

She shot me a quick glance, went on working. 'Isn't it enough?'

'Let's go somewhere we can talk about it.'

She ducked out from beneath the ramp, jerked her head at the mechanic. 'Be good fellas, will you?' she said. 'Beat it. My friend and I wanna talk.'

She ducked back underneath the car as they drifted away, continued disconnecting broken couplings.

'Could it have been done during the day?' I asked.

'Jimmy's around most of the day,' she told me, grunting with the effort of twisting another nut.

'How about at night? Anyone on duty?'

'You ever seen a night garage attendant on duty?' she shot back. 'You could steal all the cars while he's curled up asleep in his office and he wouldn't know a thing about it until morning.'

'You're taking this too lightly,' I warned. 'This is serious. You mighta been killed, instead of just crumpling your wing against the garage wall.'

'It was a beer truck,' she corrected.

'You must have some idea who's responsible.'

'No idea at all,' she said disinterestedly.

'Listen,' I growled. 'D'you have to keep working at that? Come out here and talk to me. Let the mechanic do that work.'

She gave me a frosty glance. 'No mechanic ever touches my car,' she said indignantly. 'Anything needs doing, I do myself. I don't want any ham-handed mechanic jiggering up my engine.'

'For heaven's sake leave it,' I pleaded. 'This is serious. In my opinion we should go to the police right away.'

She ducked out from under the car immediately, stood staring at me, strangely beautiful despite the smudge of oil on her cheek and her dishevelled hair. In her hand she held one of the brake couplings. 'Why the hell d'you think I asked you come look at this?' she demanded.

'You tell me.'

There was a faintly puzzled expression in her eyes like she couldn't understand my attitude. 'You left your card,' she said. 'You said if I wanted help ...'

'You sure need help, lady.'

'That's it then,' she said. 'What do I do?'

'Go tell the cops,' I advised. 'This is the second time someone's tried to murder you. You've gotta get protection.'

She scowled. Deep down in her eyes I could see the danger signals for an impending gust of anger.

'The cops are the only ones who can give you the kinda protection you require,' I insisted.

Her eyes narrowed as she said fiercely: 'I want the cops to keep outta my hair. I won't have them near me. I won't have anything to do with them. Keep the cops outta this.'

'For your own sake, I've gotta tell the cops,' I told her. 'If you won't look after yourself, I've got to do it for you.'

Her face was white with anger. She said through her teeth: 'If you dare tell them it won't do any good.'

'I've got to tell them,' I said crisply.

'I'll deny it.'

I glanced to the far end of the garage where the attendant and mechanic were talking together. She knew what was in my mind. 'They'll say anything I tell them.'

I looked down at the brake coupling in her hand. She knew the answer to that also. 'By the time you get back with the cops, there'll be new brake couplings fitted.'

'This is the second attempt,' I told her. 'How can you be so crazy?' I sighed. 'This fella's gonna try a third time. Maybe next time he'll succeed.'

'What are you trying to do, scare me?' she sneered.

I was suddenly remembering the way she'd dived her plane almost into the ground. It wasn't likely anything could scare this dame.

'Who is it?' I demanded. 'What have they got against you?'

She studied me carefully. 'You don't believe me when say I don't know, do you?'

'No,' I said bluntly.

She shrugged her shoulders. 'Nothing more to be done then.'

'There is,' I said. 'We can get the cops working on this, track this fella down, nail him before he makes a successful attempt.'

'Are you going to help me?' she asked directly.

I looked deep into her eyes, tried to read her mind. 'What do you want me to do?'

'That's what I want to know,' she retorted. 'What do I do?'

'Tell the cops.'

She stared at me, fingers working at her sides. 'Okay, Mr Janson,' she snarled. 'Scram, will ya? Blow. Beat it. Get to hell out of here.'

'I want you should come to the cops with me,' I said obstinately. 'I'm worried about you.'

'Just scram, and quit worrying.'

'I'm worried about you,' I repeated. 'You're a nice kid. I don't want anything to happen to you.'

I could see her conflicting emotions reflected in her hazel eyes. A kinda gratefulness and pleasure mingled with obstinacy and anger. The anger won. She spun on her heel, strode across to the tool bench, picked up a grease-gun. At the same time she switched on the compressor. 'You know what this is?' she demanded, breathing hard, eyes narrowed.

I knew what it was. It was a cylinder loaded with a coupla pounds of thick, black grease. She had only to press the trigger and black grease would be ejected from the muzzle with all the velocity that two hundred pounds pressure per square inch of compressed air could give it. And that was plenty. It wouldn't kill me. But it would knock me off my feet, coat me from head to toe in thick grease.

I licked my lips nervously. You couldn't tell with a dame like her. She might decide to use it whatever I said or did.

'Get moving,' she said grimly. 'I'll give you five seconds.'

'Just listen to me for a moment, honey ...' I began.

'One,' she said in a hard, detached voice. She was gonna do it. She wouldn't hesitate to do it. She was in that kinda mood.

'Okay, Beryl,' I said quietly. I tipped my fedora to the back of my head, half-turned from her, lit a cigarette.

'Two,' she counted ominously.

I turned my back on her, slowly walked to the far end of the garage and the exit. I didn't look over my shoulder once. But I sensed she was still standing there, grease-fun levelled, ready to use it if I turned back.

I didn't turn back. I went straight on out of the garage into the busy, teeming streets of Chicago, where any one of those that brushed shoulders with me on the pavement coulda been the one who calmly and murderously was planning to kill her.

And as I walked away, left her to face her danger alone, I'd learned something. Yeah, I'd learned that dame was quite a dame!

Yeah, I'd learned something else too.

I went for that dame.

8

My stupid masculine pride kept me away, and it was two days before I heard from her again. This time indirectly.

The call came through to the *Chicago Chronicle* offices and eventually caught up with me in the Newsroom.

'Mr Hank Janson?' asked the receptionist.

'That's me.'

'This is Central Hospital. Just hold on a moment, please.'

It was the Ward Sister: 'A young lady, one of our patients, wants to see you urgently. I should be pleased if you could manage to visit her.'

I figured it was some hysterical screwball dame. 'What's her name?' I asked wearily.

The Ward Sister's voice was worried, almost offended. 'She refuses to give her name. That's why if you come down here you might help put our records straight.'

I began to sweat. 'What's she look like?' I asked feverishly. 'Give me a description of her.'

There was a moment's silence. 'She's medium-sized, slim built, dark, rather longish hair ...'

'Hazel coloured eyes,' I interrupted.

'That's right,' she said. 'She also has a very hasty disposition, a little difficult to get along with ...'

'How bad is she?' I asked huskily. 'What's happened to her?'

'There's nothing to worry about at all,' she reassured me

cheerfully. 'Don't upset yourself on that account. As far as we know, she was knocked down by a car. But it's nothing serious. Certainly nothing to worry about, and ...'

'I'm on my way,' I told her, and slammed down the receiver.

It couldn't have been serious. The hospital staff were more interested in completing their record cards and entering her name and address.

I declined to give them information. 'It's up to her,' I told them. 'If she wants to keep her identity a secret, that's her business.'

'But the record cards,' wailed the white-coated records girl. 'We must have full details.'

I turned to the Ward Sister. 'You know I can't give information without her permission. Where is she? Let me see her.' The Ward Sister primly led me along corridors, past long wards with their neat, white cots.

'We've put her in a private room,' she explained. Then she added, cautiously: 'She's very temperamental, you know. She's inclined to be a little tiresome.'

'I can guess,' I said drily.

Beryl sure looked tiresome. When the Ward Sister opened the door, she was sitting bolt upright in bed, her black hair falling down over her shoulders and looking even morn bluey-black against the white hospital nightgown that was several sizes too large for her. There was an ice-pack on her head, held in position by a thick, white bandage. But despite that she was in good form, eyes glinting angrily, brows furrowed in temper.

'Give me my clothes,' she stormed, as soon as she caught sight of the Ward Sister's face. Then she kinda relaxed when she saw me. 'Thank heavens you've arrived!' Her tone suggested I was an employee who shoulda arrived an hour ago.

Discreetly the Ward Sister beckoned me past her, backed out and shut the door behind her. I took off my fedora, lounged across to the bed, sat on the edge of it.

'Go after her,' she commanded. 'Make her bring me my

clothes.'

'Relax,' I drawled. 'Take it easy. There's plenty of time. What's been going on?'

'I had to ask them to phone you,' she said resentfully, as though she'd hated them doing it. 'They won't give me my clothes and you're the only one I know who can help.'

'Take it slowly, take it from the beginning and tell me everything,' I encouraged.

'Gimme a cigarette,' she said with a curl of her lips.

I glanced up at the notice on the wall printed in thick red letters stating smoking was prohibited.

'To hell with that,' she snarled. 'Gimme a cigarette before I go crazy.'

I gave her a cigarette. It helped. She relaxed back against the pillows, settled herself more comfortably, puffed smoke at the ceiling.

'They told me it was a car accident,' I said.

She grinned at me impishly, almost delightedly. 'Third failure,' she said.

It may have been funny to her. It wasn't to me. 'How did it happen?'

She shrugged disinterestedly. 'Amateurish attempt, this time. Musta been following me in his car. As I got out of mine, he put his foot on the throttle, tried to run me down.'

'Did you see him? Did you get a glimpse of him? Did you see the licence plate?'

She was laughing at me openly now, hazel eyes warm with amusement. 'Listen, Bighead,' she chuckled. 'The next time you catch a glimpse of a car from the corner of your eye that's hurtling towards you at full speed, see if you get time to read number plates.'

'But afterwards,' I said. 'After he'd gone past, didn't you see his number?'

She turned on her side, ruefully fingered her haunch through the bedclothes. 'Use your imagination, Bighead,' she drawled. 'If I hadn't jumped, I'd have been mincemeat by now. The car wing caught me right here.' She tapped her haunch and winced humorously. 'It's the hardest kick in the pants I've ever had. It spun me round a coupla times and I cracked the back of my head when I hit the ground. The next I knew was when I awoke in the blood wagon with one hell of a headache.'

'How's the head now?' I asked sympathetically.

'I'm okay,' she said impatiently. 'A lump the size of a boiled egg, but it won't kill me. All I want is to get out of this joint. If they don't bring my clothes soon, I'm gonna raise all hell with the Board of Directors.'

'You look cute sitting there with that ice bag on your nut,' I told her. 'That's a cute nightie, too. You should be comfortable here.'

She glared at me. 'Are you gonna help me or not?'

I shrugged my shoulders. 'What can I do?'

'Get my clothes for me. Get me outta here.'

'They wanna know your name,' I told her. 'They want your address. Why are you holding out on them?'

'Because I don't want damned cops snooping around asking questions.'

I got up. 'It might not be a bad idea at that.'

Her eyes narrowed angrily. 'You're a real four flusher,' she sneered. 'Twice I've asked you to help. Twice you've backed down on me. Don't you feel proud of yourself!'

Her voice was loaded with contempt. Each of her words stung me. I sat on the edge of the bed again. 'Listen, honey,' I said. 'Someone's trying to kill you. Can't you get that into your head? I don't want anything to happen to you.'

'I know what I'm doing,' she snapped. 'I'm asking just one favour from you. Help me get out of here. I need someone's signature who'll be responsible for seeing I get home. Do that much for me, will you?'

I got up. 'Okay,' I agreed reluctantly. 'But I don't make a nickel out of it.'

'I'll pay you,' she snapped coolly.

'I've got dough,' I told her.

She stared at me, then lowered her eyes. She was thinking

the same as me. It had come into both our minds at he same instant.

'If you're not feeling too bad from that crack on the head, maybe you'll join me at dinner tonight,' I suggested gently.

She still wouldn't look at me. 'That might be nice,' she said, as though she doubted it.

'I'll go get your clothes,' I told her.

It was the same rig-out, the blue jeans, the windjammer and the yellow sweater, all very dusty and very much the worse for being rolled in the gutter.

I waited downstairs while she got dressed, and signed an undertaking to make sure she got home safely. Then I escorted her to my car, got her settled comfortably beside the driving seat and went around the other side, got down behind the driving wheel.

As soon as the car started, she stripped off the bandage they'd wound around her head, fingered the sore place tenderly. 'Sure must have dented the pavement,' she told me.

'Seems like your head is as hard as your heart.'

She shot me a stern glance. 'You can cut out those cracks. There's nothing wrong with my heart.'

'No-one will ever know unless they get real close to it.'

'I'm close to it,' she said. 'I know.'

'You figure you knowing is sufficient?'

'Cut out the fancy talk,' she snarled. 'Okay, so you made a pass at me that made me schoolgirlish. I'm not denying it. But that's ancient history. It's finished now. Forget the gooey stuff, because I don't want any of it.'

'What are you afraid of?'

She stared at me insolently. 'I'm not afraid of anything. I just don't like guys who figure a dame's something pleasant to maul around when they're in the mood.'

'When who's in the mood?' I asked. 'The dame or the guy?'

She flushed. 'Skip it.'

'Sure, if that's what you want.'

We hardly spoke another word until we got to her apartment. She unlocked the door. I stood outside, politely waiting to be invited to a drink. She said haughtily: 'If you'll give me a bill, I'll pay your petrol expenses and the time you wasted.'

She was trying to get me mad. It was almost a calculated insult. I suppressed my anger, smiled suavely. 'I'll have an invoice with me when I call tonight,' I told her.

She was closing the door in my face. Her eyebrows arched. 'When you call tonight?'

'The dinner arrangement,' I gently reminded her. 'My terms for getting you out of the hospital.'

She scowled. 'You want to hold me to it?'

'Not if you want to evade your obligations.'

'I agreed,' she snarled. 'I'll keep my promise.'

'That's good,' I said with satisfaction. 'And by the way. Don't forget to loosen your braces tonight. Since you were dunked, your pants have shrunk and become tight under the armpits.'

I stood grinning at the smooth panels of the slammed door, then turned slowly, made my way back to the street.

I was worried about that dame. Three attempts to kill her, three savage and brutal attempts.

She was a difficult dame to help, but a dinner date would give me the opportunity of keeping near her, watching for a lead to the unknown and as yet unsuccessful killer.

9

It was good mental exercise figuring where to dine a dame who has a yen for jeans and a windjammer.

South Side, where could be seen the existentialists who roamed the streets and frequented the cafes, the manly-looking dames wearing trousers and sweaters puffing at cigarettes that drooped from thick lips, and long-haired guys in brightly-coloured sweaters and corduroys, talking in high-pitched voices and calling each other 'darling,' was a possibility.

Yeah, probably she'd have passed in that company. It was me who was the trouble. I got cold shudders running down my spine at the thought of rubbing shoulders with weak-chinned, blue-eyed, womanly-like males, who in the name of art jeopardized their manhood.

I could have taken her to the college district where the co-eds, complete with bobby-sox and rolled-up slacks, were a commonplace sight with their young, boyish, co-ed escorts. But a grown man sitting up at a cafe counter sipping milk shakes through a straw would have earned plenty of wise-cracks and jeers from the under-twenties who surrounded him.

Yeah, it took a lotta thinking to decide just exactly how one took a dame like Beryl to dinner.

I finally came up with the answer. I'd treat her the same as any other dame, take her to dinner at my favourite and fashionable grill-room, behave towards her as though she was fashionably dressed, find out just how far she could pursue happily her don't-care-a-damn-about-anyone attitude.

I made one final finger adjustment to my tie, patted my breast pocket handkerchief to ensure it didn't spoil the line of my suit, and thumbed her doorbell.

She took all of three minutes to open the door, and when she did, she opened it wide. So wide she was framed in the doorway like a life-size portrait.

I gaped.

Her hazel eyes twinkled roguishly and she flushed sweetly.

I gaped some more, kept staring, couldn't believe the transformation. It was the first time I'd seen her wearing a dress.

And what a dress!

I'd got so used to seeing her in trousers that I was kinda instantaneously drenched in her femininity. And that dress did everything to emphasize her maturity.

Fashions change from generation to generation, dress styles following the moral codes of the age. In the 17th Century, when women were freely and frankly admired for their charms, the display of their attributes became a moral necessity. In those days, a woman who wore dresses that *failed* to completely reveal her breasts was regarded as immoral and a hussy, and was shunned accordingly. During the subsequent generations, the pendulum swung to the opposite extreme, resulting in the cramping, compressing and furious corseting of the Victorian age, the long, black dresses that concealed even the ankles and trailed in the filth of the streets, picking up the germs of disease that shortly attacked the wearer of the unhygienic clothing. It resulted in high-neck dresses that fastened tightly around the throat, long sleeves that fitted tightly at the wrists, guaranteeing the wearer would be starved of air, which is breathed in through the pores of the skin as well as through the mouth. It resulted in that absurdity of all absurdities – the swim girl wading from the sea enveloped in a costume that covered her from ankle to throat, her sun-starved body cheated of the life-giving rays of the sun by the moral convention that a woman's body should not be seen.

Fortunately the pendulum is swinging back to sanity. The fact that the human body can be beautiful is becoming more and more widely recognized. Women are becoming increasingly conscious that the display of their womanliness is pleasurable as well as giving pleasure. As the moral code has changed, people are freeing themselves from the shackles of narrow-mindedness, and are accepting the basic facts of life instead of thrusting them out of sight like something unnatural, unclean and shocking. Fashions have adapted themselves to the changing ideas. The dressmakers who twenty years ago insisted upon tight bandaging to preserve their mannish, flat-chested dress styles, now mould their dresses with rounded emphasis, provide artificial curves where natural ones are lacking, and exercise inspired display ingenuity when the natural curves need no artificial aids.

Beryl's dressmaker hadn't needed any artificial aids. And her display ingenuity had certainly been inspired. American television and nightclubs during the past coupla years have presented the public nightly with a kinda unofficial competition between its most beautiful patrons as to which could show the most without showing everything.

That dress of Beryl's certainly got into the semi-finals.

I yammered, felt the palms of my hands sweating. 'You're … you're beautiful!' I burst out, conscious it was hardly a compliment at this late stage in our relationship.

She didn't need words to learn my appreciation. My eyes told her everything. She motioned me inside, closed the door behind me slowly and gracefully. The way she did it enabled me to admire her from all angles.

The dress was black velvet, a perfect setting for the warm, golden brown of her skin. The dress bared her shoulders, which was necessary because they were so beautifully rounded and fascinating. And the bodice, with the exception of the deep-boned vee in the centre, which plunged almost to her waist, was a straight line, stretching low down across her breasts so she swelled up out of it, symbolizing beauty bursting from imprisonment.

Beauty nearly made its escape!

'Let's get a drink, Bighead,' she said, and her eyes were dancing with pleased vanity because of the flattery of my eyes, my face and my reactions.

Breathless, I followed her along the corridor to the lounge, watching the smooth, easy sway of her hips, the twitch of her half-ankle-length skirt and the softness of her shoulders.

'Pour me a rye, too,' she instructed. 'I shan't be a minute now, just a little more titivating.'

I poured two shots of rye, sauntered across to the bedroom door, hesitated just outside. 'Okay if I come in?'

'Sure. I've nothing to hide.'

It was almost true. She almost had nothing to hide. I particularly noticed that when I stood over her as she sat before the dressing-table, carefully applying perfume to the lobes of her ears. There wasn't anything tight about that bodice. The bursting-from-imprisonment effect was purely natural.

'That's a nice dress you're wearing,' I said hoarsely.

'You like it, huh?' She was happy, stimulated by my appreciation.

'It's the first time I've seen you in woman's clothes.'

She nodded across the room towards the wardrobe. 'I had some more made while I was about it. Take a look.'

It was a long wardrobe stretching the length of the wall. Her dressmaker sure musta been working overtime. There was an array of dresses and gowns that would have stocked a shop. The shelves contained stacks of delicate, gossamer underclothing.

I whistled.

'Surprised, huh, Bighead?' she asked, looking at me through the mirror while she carefully pressed a stray curl into position.

'Musta cost the Earth,' I said.

'Probably did,' she said offhandedly.

I'd been wanting to ask for a long time. I asked now. 'Where d'you get that kinda dough.'

'I just get it,' she said, and her voice showed dough wasn't of the slightest interest to her. 'D'you like my shoes?'

There were maybe a coupla dozen pairs. 'Sure,' I said. 'I like.'

'Be ready in just a minute now,' she assured me.

There was a ring at the doorbell.

'I'll get it,' I said.

'Don't bother. I'll get it.'

I was through the door by now, crossing the lounge. 'It's all right,' I called over my shoulder. 'I'll get it.'

She was just behind me, reached the door as I got it open. He was a stoutish, fiftyish guy with grey hair glinting at the sides of a healthily-tanned face. He was smartly-dressed, wearing a rolled-up umbrella and a bowler hat. His blue eyes stared at me in surprise before they flicked past me to Beryl. Then his round face seemed to expand as he smiled with relief and pleasure.

'Beryl!' he said.

'Charlie!' she cried delightedly. 'You old hound. What are you doing here? What a wonderful surprise.'

I was suddenly forgotten, kinda edged to one side by her as she took him by the arm, clung to him, hustled him along the corridor to the lounge.

I glowered, closed the door and trailed after them.

'So good to see you, Charlie,' she thrilled as she pushed him down on the settee, whisked the umbrella from his protesting grasp, pulled off his hat and playfully rumpled his hair. 'You old devil,' she giggled. 'Why didn't you tell me you were in town?'

'That's it, Beryl,' he said. 'I couldn't. I didn't know where you were. I heard about the explosion and ...'

'I'll get you a drink,' she said. 'I'll mix it just the way you like it.'

She danced across to the cocktail cabinet, began pouring

and mixing. 'How long you been in town?' she asked over her shoulder.

'Got in this morning,' he told her. 'Devil of a job finding where you were.'

She'd mixed his drink by now. She took it over to him, stood staring down at him, her face alight with pleasure. 'Let me have a good look at you,' she thrilled. She scrutinized his face carefully. 'It's the same old Charlie,' she enthused. I must give you a big squeeze.' She sat on his lap to do it, wrapped her bare arms around his neck, gave him a big, vigorous hug.

Chuckling, he put his arms around her, one fat, short-fingered hand around her waist, the other resting on her hip as he squeezed her tightly.

I was understanding slowly, and it wasn't pleasant to understand. Charlie obviously had dough, probably enough dough to pay for all those dresses in the wardrobe. I cleared my throat. I said hoarsely, gratingly: 'Looks like you're kinda busy, Miss Pinder. We'll skip our date. I'll just push off.'

She looked up, as though remembering for the first time I was there. 'Don't be silly, Bighead,' she snapped. 'We don't need to break a date on account of Charlie. Charlie don't mind, do you, darling?' She pinched his cheek. Then she suddenly remembered. 'Of course, you two haven't met yet. Hank, meet Charlie,'

He beamed at me good-naturedly, nodded a greeting. I glowered at him and grunted.

'Oh, be nice to Charlie,' she told me poutingly. 'Say hello to him properly.'

I glowered some more, grunted, 'Hiya,' in the tone of voice that meant *go-to-hell*.

She gave Charlie a playful little kiss, got up off his lap, straightened out her skirt. 'Hank's taking me to dinner tonight,' she explained. 'I'll have to see you later on tonight. Now you two boys have a chat while I finish my titivating.'

She slipped into the bedroom and I stood glaring at Charlie, undecided whether I should walk out right away. I hadn't liked that crack about seeing him later that night.

He beamed at me, his smile slowly changing to one of concern. He cleared his throat. 'Blowing up a bit,' he said awkwardly.

I stared at him. 'Yeah,' I grunted.

There was a long silence.

'You live in Chicago?' he asked.

'Yup.'

Another long silence. He made another effort. 'Known Beryl long?'

'What the hell's that to do with you?' I demanded fiercely. My tone was so savage, he half-flinched. His blue eyes widened, blinked his surprise.

His reaction made all of it more sickening. He hadn't flared back at me. He wasn't mad the way I was mad. Instead, he'd acted his age, acted like an old guy of fifty or more who could buy a dame, have her pet him and suck up to him.

I finished my drink quickly, reached for my fedora. 'Say, you're not going,' he asked in a tone of disapproval.

'That's just what I'm doing,' I snarled.

'But Beryl,' he protested. 'You were going to ...'

'I've lost my appetite,' I snarled. 'Present her my excuses, tell her I've remembered something really important I wanna do.'

He called loudly. 'Just a minute. Beryl!'

She got to the door of the bedroom as I reached the door of the lounge. Instinctively with woman's intuition she realized what was happening.

'Bighead!' she called commandingly.

I stopped, turned around to face her. There was injured anger in her eyes. 'Just where d'you think you're going?'

'Listen, lady,' I snarled. 'I don't want to interfere with your private plans. There's other things I can do.'

'You big dope,' she flared.

'That's what I'm beginning to realize,' I retorted.

Charlie got up. There was understanding dawning in his eyes. 'Now listen, son,' he began heavily.

'Keep out of this,' I growled. 'I don't know you. I don't

wanna know you.'

'Let him go if he wants, Charlie,' she said. She was furious.

'Be fair to him,' Charlie said. 'It's natural. He doesn't understand.'

'Why should he need to understand?' she snapped. 'Let him go, if that's what he thinks.'

'Look, son,' he said pacifically. 'You've got it wrong. It's not what you think. I'm her father.'

I flushed to the roots of my hair. I could see it all then She was the kinda dame who would call her father Charlie. If ever a guy felt foolish, it was me right then.

Charlie stepped in quickly, smoothed over the awkwardness that was a barrier between me and Beryl. 'I'll get you another drink,' he said, bustling to the cocktail cabinet, clinking ice into a glass.

She stared at me frostily.

I stared back.

'That wasn't a very pleasant thing to think,' she snapped.

I went a shade more crimson. 'I'm sorry, Beryl,' I said huskily. 'But the way you acted, it looked just ...'

Charlie turned back from the cocktail cabinet, gave me my drink. 'Now, now,' he said pacifically. 'Don't you two start fighting. You go out and enjoy yourselves.'

'You come with us, Charlie,' she invited, giving me a malicious glare.

'Wouldn't dream of it,' he said. 'Too many things to do.' He gave me a sly wink that she couldn't see. 'I've got plenty on my own plate.'

'I'm sorry, Beryl,' I said humbly. 'Let's get going, huh?'

She stood there undecided, said reluctantly: 'I guess I can't back out now.'

There were angry words rushing to my lips, but already he was taking her by the arm, steering her towards the bedroom. 'That's right, honey,' he said. 'You go get yourself dolled up. You and me can have a talk later.'

She disappeared inside the bedroom, closed the door behind her. He looked at me, winked.

I liked him. He'd suddenly ceased to be a lecherous old sugar daddy and had become benevolent and fatherly.

He said quietly. 'Known Beryl long?'

'A few days.'

He nodded. Then he frowned. 'What's behind this explosion that happened in her flat?'

I shot a quick glance at the bedroom door, finished my drink, stepped right close to him and took him by the arm. 'Listen,' I said grimly. 'You're her father. You ought to know about this. She's in trouble, real trouble. Somebody's gunning for her, and she won't tell the cops.'

His eyes widened, stared disbelievingly.

'She won't help herself, somebody's gotta do something about it,' I said. 'You can help. Who do you know who would want to see her wind up in the morgue?'

His eyes were suspicious. He licked his lips nervously. 'You're kinda rushing me, son,' he said. 'I haven't got a grip on this yet. Just what are you trying to tell me?'

'Listen,' I gritted, clenching his arm tightly. 'Someone sent her a trick parcel. It destroyed her apartment, would have blown her to pieces. A coupla days later, the brake couplings on her car were filed through. She hit a beer truck but was lucky a second time. A coupla days after that, she barely jumped clear of a car that tried to run her down. Someone's trying to kill her, I tell you.'

His eyes were wide and solemn. 'That's crazy. Who would want to do that?'

I almost danced with impatience. 'That's what I'm trying to find out,' I gritted. 'You're her father. You ought to know, if anyone. Who is in town who would want to bump her off?'

His eyes were still suspicious. 'Even if what you say is true, I wouldn't know. She moved into Chicago three or four weeks ago. Her first time here. I wouldn't know if she's made any enemies.'

I thought that over for a long time. 'What's she doing here anyway?'

He coughed, looked down at his shoes, avoided my eyes.

'We're kinda primitive back where we come from,' he admitted grudgingly. 'Seems like three or four of the local youngsters figured they had an equal calling right on Beryl. Competition became pretty high, until the four were all for fighting a duel to sort things out.'

'Maybe it's one of the losers gunning for her,' I put in quickly.

He shrugged his shoulders. 'There's no way of telling. Beryl lit out before they got started. She didn't want any of them, on no account. Said if they wanted to shoot up each other like crazy men, it was no concern of hers. She just didn't want anything to do with any of them.'

'That's why she came to Chicago?'

'I guess so.'

'Who else knew she was in Chicago?'

'Just me, I guess.'

I heard her hand on the door handle. 'I've got to see you later,' I whispered quickly. 'Where can I get you?'

'Randolph Hotel.'

'I'll be there.' Then I switched my eyes to the doorway, feasted them on Beryl as she came through, a pure, milk-white fur cape draped over her beautiful shoulders.

Any guy would have felt proud to take her anywhere. I took her to my favourite grill-room, basked in the envious glances of guys I knew who just couldn't switch their eyes away when Beryl eased that cape back from off her shoulders and allowed her charm to radiate a magic aura around our table.

Conversation was strained at first. Then, by the time we got to the main dish and were halfway through the bottle of champagne, we mellowed, were talking like old friends, enjoyed an intimate harmony of mind that was strangely pleasing.

After the cabaret show, when the lights had gone up and the table was cleared for coffee and brandy, it was like we had known each other all our lives. It was the kinda atmosphere that enabled me to ask questions without them seeming rude.

'Your father's a nice guy,' I said.

Her eyes twinkled expressively. 'He's fun,' she agreed.

I twirled my brandy glass between my fingers. I was thinking of the vast quantities of dough she handled so nonchalantly. 'Looks after you well,' I commented.

'Yes. He's a darling. He couldn't be any better if he was my father.'

I froze. I stopped twirling the glass, said without looking up at her: 'Isn't he your father?'

She chuckled. 'Don't start getting ideas, Hank. Of course he's my father. My step-father.'

I absorbed that slowly, let it sink deep down into my consciousness. 'Your father's dead then?'

She nodded slowly. 'It happened when I was twelve.'

'Your mother? Is she still alive?'

She shook her head slowly, almost sadly. 'Charlie's all I've got now.'

'Done rather well for himself, hasn't he?'

She nodded, like it was a question to which she herself had previously given consideration. 'I guess he has.'

'Doesn't seem to keep you short of dough?'

She chuckled musically. 'He doesn't have to. When mother died, I inherited everything. The oil wells, the plant, the estate, everything there was. She willed it all to me.'

Something in my brain began to tick. 'What does Charlie do? I mean, if everything was left to you, where did Charlie come in?'

'Oh, Charlie's wonderful,' she enthused. 'He looks after everything for me, runs the refinery, organizes production, markets the finished product. He does everything!'

'And everything belongs to you,' I persisted.

She looked at me curiously. 'But it doesn't make any difference,' she explained. 'Actually it belongs to both of us. Charlie can have anything he wants.'

I finished my brandy, refilled my glass and stared at it steadily. 'Just supposing,' I said. 'Just suppose you'd been in the apartment when that bomb exploded. What would have happened to your property?'

Her eyes had hardened. She suspected what was behind my question, but couldn't be certain. 'Charlie gets everything, I guess,' she said quietly.

'You've willed everything to him?' I asked.

'My mother did,' she said. 'Dad left everything to Mum, Mum left everything to me. But if I don't get married and if anything happens to me, Charlie gets it.'

The words were trembling on my tongue. I wanted to say: 'Can you be sure of Charlie? Don't you know how guys are when a lot of money is at stake? Don't you realize some guys would kill for a dollar?' But there was suspicion and a warning in her eyes. She had no doubts whatsoever. And to voice my doubts would break up an enjoyable evening.

I dug down in my pocket, pulled out my cigarette case, offered it to her. She leaned forward across the table, selected a cigarette carefully, placed it between her lips and leaned even further across the table towards my lighter. With that low bodice, there was no more delightful position she could pose than that of bending forward to me that way.

She flushed shyly, smiled with embarrassed pleasure. 'You are a beast, Hank,' she chided. 'Unfair, too. It's unfair the way you look. It makes me ... don't keep doing it. There's people watching.'

'A cat can look at a queen,' I told her.

'You're not a cat. You're a wolf.'

'I like you dressed this way,' I told her.

'I imagine so,' she said drily, 'judging from the way you're using your eyes.'

'I don't necessarily mean that. I mean I like you when you're human, when you're dressed like a woman, behaving like a woman.'

Her eyes narrowed the tiniest bit. 'You like women to be soft and clinging,' she said softly. But there was a hint of challenge in her voice too. 'You like women to be feminine, to look up to their menfolk, listen eagerly to everything a man says and agree with it. You think women are inferior, incapable of doing things men can do. You think ...'

She was lashing herself into highly-strung, emotional indignation. I still didn't want the evening spoiled.

'What d'you think you're proving by wearing jeans and a windjammer,' I demanded. 'Sure, go ahead and wear them. Make yourself as unromantic-looking as a man. Prove you can fly a plane, drive a car, doctor an engine, walk like a man. Sure, go ahead and prove it. Where does get you? I guess nine women out of ten could do all those things if they wanted. The smart thing is not to want to do them. Because having proved you can do them, it's got you nowhere.'

'It gives satisfaction to prove women can do the things men can do.'

'Who to? A woman? Certainly to no-one else. And the dame who does the things men do will one day feel almighty miserable when she discovers her men friends regard her as just another fella instead of a woman who needs a little affection and necking.'

Maybe she needed the jeans and windjammer to give her moral support. Maybe wearing them she'd have behaved differently. Maybe then she'd have pulled the joint apart. As it was, she rose swiftly to her feet, with hard and glinting eyes. 'I think you'd better take me home,' she said icily.

You can't argue with a dame who's standing on her feet. Not when every other guy in the restaurant whom you know is watching. I got up, smirked around uneasily to show nothing was wrong, lay some dollar bills on the table and followed her as she glided to the foyer with a queenly dignity and grace.

The commissionaire hailed a taxi, and I thoughtfully adjusted her fur cape around her shoulders against the night air. I gave the driver her address, climbed into the cab the alongside her.

Maybe my comments about her discovering guys were thinking of her as a woman got her worried. Maybe she figured she ought to check up to make sure she wasn't losing ground.

As for me, well I'd been sitting opposite that low-cut dress all through dinner with my senses of sight, smell and touch being stimulated overtime. I just couldn't resist giving her the opportunity to slap me down. And she didn't!

I'd never known a taxi journey seem so short when I was footing the bill. It seemed no time before he was braking outside her apartment. It caught us both by surprise. I leaned forward, blocked the driver's view while she thrust and pushed herself back within the bounds proposed by her dress designer.

'It's a couple of bucks,' the driver told me. I fumbled for the dough with sweaty hands, found that even the sound of her heavy breathing was getting me more excited.

'You getting out here, Bud?' asked the driver as I gave him the dough and an ample tip.

'That's the general idea.'

'Your face, Bud,' he said. 'Your face!'

I glanced in the mirror, rubbed vigorously with my hand-kerchief. I had to switch the light on to do it. Her face was flushed, her eyes shy and embarrassed. She patted her dishevelled hair into shape with one hand, held her white fur cape closely around her shoulders with the other.

It couldn't end this way, not for either of us. This was like an avalanche, a tiny pebble of feeling that had become an onrushing mass of overpowering emotions that couldn't be stemmed.

Neither of us spoke as the elevator hop whisked us to her floor level. I held her arm tightly, felt her trembling. We didn't have to talk. She knew this was *it*, the same as I did. There were all kinds of thoughts running through my mind. I wanted this to be everything it should be. I wanted it to be something really beautiful, something wonderful. But I knew so little about her, was afraid of doing the wrong thing, destroying everything.

The elevator hop opened the doors, and she swayed against me as she stepped outside. She was breathing deeply, almost panting, and by the trembling of her arm I could tell she was as hot as hell.

Then, as the elevator doors closed behind us, I felt her tense, felt frustration sweep over me in an angry flood.

It was Charlie. A beaming, self-satisfied Charlie, waiting in the corridor outside her apartment. And there was nothing we could do about it. He had seen us. She hesitated momentarily like she was wondering if we could turn around, go away some place where we could be alone. But he waved cheerfully, made a wry face to show he had been waiting a long time.

Hot the way she was, she didn't want Charlie around any more than I did. 'I'd have got in touch with you tomorrow,' she told him irritably as she opened the door.

'Couldn't miss having a nightcap with you, my dear,' he said benevolently, pushing in front of me, following her through into the apartment.

I closed the door behind me, wanted to help her off with her wrap. Charlie beat me to it. I glared at the back of his head.

'Oh, let me, darling,' he said cheerfully, leading the way through to the lounge like he owned it and beating her to the cocktail cabinet.

Her hazel eyes flashed me a look of hopeless despair. Her bare shoulders shrugged a little note of unhappiness. 'Small brandy for me, Charlie,' she said dully.

We stood around the cocktail cabinet while he mixed the drinks. She kept looking at me and I kept looking at her. It was like we couldn't take our eyes off each other. I was racking my brain for some plausible reason I should give him for getting the hell out of it. Beryl wasn't that tactful. 'You must be tired, Charlie,' she said. 'All that travelling, too. You must get some rest. I'll call a taxi for you as soon as you've finished your brandy.'

'But I'm not tired, my dear,' he protested. Then he caught on. He looked from her to me and gave an artful chuckle, wagged a remonstrating forefinger. 'Now, you young things,' he said playfully.

He didn't strike the right note. Somehow he seemed to make everything ugly and cold-blooded. Beryl abruptly turned her shoulders on him.

He didn't please me either. I said icily: 'I think she's right. You look tired. You ought to finish that brandy quickly.'

He looked from me to her bare shoulders, then back again. He gave a sickly grin. 'Maybe you're right,' he said.

There was dead silence then, a waiting silence.

He was finishing his drink, gulping it too quickly. If ever a guy musta felt awkward, it was him. 'I'll ring for a taxi,' he said at last.

'It's not late,' said Beryl without turning around. 'You'll catch one outside easily.'

He took out a gold watch, studied it earnestly. 'I don't know,' he doubted. 'It's safer to ring.'

'There's plenty outside,' said Beryl irritably. She strode to the window, pulled back the thick velvet curtains. She was there for maybe ten seconds, looking down into the street. 'I've seen three pass already,' she announced. 'You won't have any trouble, Charlie. You'll be able to catch one right away.'

'Very well, my dear,' he said pacifically. 'If you're not busy, perhaps you'll give me a ring at the hotel in the morning and ...'

It was like a single, sharp tap on glass with a small hammer. The whistle and the dull thud as lead ploughed into woodwork was punctuated by a short, sharp gasp of surprise and fright from Beryl.

For maybe a second, there was stunned surprise. Then my numbed reflexes came into action. I lunged for the light switch, plunged the room into darkness, yelled to Beryl to keep away from the window, and stumbled through to the bedroom, barking my shins against furniture as I made for the window.

I pulled back the curtain cautiously. I knew whoever had fired that shot would be watching the lounge window. But just the same, there was no point in taking needless chances. The would-be murderer wasn't taking needless chances either. A small, black saloon parked opposite was jolting into movement even as I caught sight of it. A hunched-up figure crouching over the driving wheel was enveloped in shadow and, as I threw up the sash, peered after the car, I knew I was wasting my time. The number-plate had been carefully obscured with mud.

I switched on the bedroom light, walked through to the lounge, switched on the light. Beryl was standing against the wall, well away from the window, her face white and her eyes hard and glinting with anger. I sure admired her in that moment. It was probably the closest she'd come to death in her life and she had the guts to get mad about it instead of hysterical.

I strode across to the window, examined the neat, round hole punched through it as cleanly as though it had been made with a diamond drill. I became conscious of Charlie staring at it over my shoulder.

'Someone shot at her,' he said incredulously.

'You catch on,' I grunted. Then, in case the killer took into his head to tour the block and have a second shot, I jerked the curtains across the window.

Beryl said in a low, suppressed voice: 'When I get my hands on that fella, I'll ...'

Charlie said incredulously: 'It was a bullet. Somebody tried to kill you, honey.'

'The fourth time in succession,' I said grimly, and strode across to the far side of the room where the splintered door frame showed where the spent bullet had embedded itself. I took out my penknife, probed at it, pried it loose.

Charlie was standing beside me again, incredulous eyes watching everything I was doing. 'This is it,' I said grimly. 'For the first time, we've got a lead. Ballistics department will be able to identify the gun that fired this bullet.'

Beryl said in a cold voice: 'I told you, Hank. Keep the cops outta this. They're a meddling lot of fools. I won't have them sticking their long noses into my affairs, prying into my private life. Keep the cops out of this.'

I stared at her levelly. 'Not this time, honey,' I said. 'I'm getting the cops whether you like it or not. You can shout your head off, but that's what I'm doing.'

Charlie's wide, disbelieving eyes were fastened on my hand. 'Let me have a look at that,' he pleaded.

Beryl came right over to me, eyes narrowed and glinting dangerously. 'Don't you dare!' she threatened. 'Don't you dare!'

I was waging a psychological battle with her. I was only vaguely conscious of Charlie prying open my fingers, taking the spent bullet and examining it. 'You can't fight the cops all the time, Beryl,' I told her. 'Okay. Maybe you did get a raw deal from them. Personally, I don't think you did. But even so, you've got a right to police protection the same as any other citizen.'

'I don't want police protection,' she stormed. 'I want protection *from* the police.'

'You're gonna hate me for this, honey,' I said. 'But I've gotta do it.' I pushed past her, walked to the telephone. She made no attempt to stop me, instead she swiftly seized a cushion, ran to the window. I stared as she pulled back the curtains, rested the cushion against the punctured glass and hammered with her fist until the tinkling of broken glass warned the pane had been smashed.

She turned and faced me defiantly. 'Now try telling the police,' she flared. 'What proof have you got?'

There was still the bullet hole in the doorpost. I said nothing and picked up the telephone as she rushed through to the kitchen. I wondered what was in her mind as I joggled the receiver rest impatiently. I still hadn't got through to the operator when she got back with an ice-pick.

I was slow off the mark. She'd hacked at the doorway, splintered it, obliterated most of the signs of the bullet hole before I wrested the axe from her. It was lucky I got it from her. She was so worked up by this time she'd have as soon embedded it in my skull as in the doorpost.

'Get out,' she stormed. 'Get out of here.'

Charlie was gaping, wide-eyed and uncomprehending. She twisted herself from my grasp, rushed at him, snatched the bullet from his unprotesting hands.

She was out-thinking me all the way along the line. Calling the cops wasn't gonna do me any good, because all the evidence left to prove my story was a broken window pane and a hacked doorpost.

I needed that bullet. Yeah, I needed that bullet badly. I advanced on her, hand extended. 'Give,' I rasped.

She was a woman and she had something to hide. She did what most women do instinctively under such circumstances. She thrust it in the bodice of her dress.

I stood staring at her, breathing hard, knowing full well if Charlie hadn't been there I'd have got my hands on that piece of evidence even if my face had been clawed to pieces in the process.

'Get out,' she snarled.

'I'm not going,' I said determinedly. 'I'm staying. I'm not leaving you alone. Not after what's happened. I'm not leaving until I've got what I'm after.'

'Get out,' she snarled. 'Get out or I'll call the manager and have you thrown out.'

'I'm not leaving you here alone,' I said doggedly. 'Not after what's just happened.'

Charlie's bewildered face swam into my vision. 'Listen,' he said urgently. 'You realize what this means. Someone is trying to kill her.'

'She's trying to meet him halfway,' I rasped.

He turned to Beryl. 'You ought to do what the young fella suggests,' he told her.

'You keep out of this, Charlie,' she ordered. 'This is my affair,'

'Beryl,' he pleaded. 'You can't stop here alone, not after what's happened.'

I was remembering all the very good reasons Charlie might have for disposing of Beryl. 'I'm staying,' I said. 'I'm not letting you out of my sight.'

She stood there, beautiful and feminine, breasts high and proud, eyes flaming with anger. 'I'm not a child,' she stormed. 'I can look after myself. You can both clear out. Both of you!'

'I want that bullet,' I said steadily.

She tossed her head at me, stalked from the lounge, along the corridor to the outer door. She opened it, held it wide. 'Outside,' she said crisply. 'Both of you. Outside, or I'll have you put out.'

I dug my heels into the carpet, stood there with feet astride, determined not to move.

Charlie edged up alongside me, took my arm. He whispered in an undertone. 'We can't do anything while she's in this mood. Let her have her own way for the present. I wanna talk this over with you.'

Instinctively I realized the truth of what he said. No-one could reason with her while she was in this mood. Wordlessly I crossed the room, strode along the corridor and out through the door. Charlie followed closely behind, his short legs working overtime to keep pace with mine.

'What a girl,' he said, wincing as the slammed door impacted his eardrums.

'She's crazy,' I said. 'Like a cask of dynamite. You can't reason with her.'

'We're different,' he said. 'We're men. We can get together quietly, talk this thing over calmly.'

I studied him carefully. I retained my suspicions of him, but a man can't be in two places at one time. Of one thing I was quite certain. It wasn't Charlie who'd taken a shot at Beryl.

'There's a bar opposite,' I suggested. 'Let's go get a beer.'

We became real thick over our third beer. Charlie was as worried as me about Beryl. He suggested practical angles.

'She's been like it all her life,' he told me. 'She's so accustomed to getting her own way, she just has to have it any time she wants – or else! You can't break her. You've got to humour her, lead her. I know, because I've had her around me since she wore pigtails. You've got to handle her gently and discreetly.'

'Right now,' I reminded him, 'she's in that apartment by herself. Four attempts have already been made on her life. Just what do you intend to do about it!'

He said slowly. 'She's got a grudge against the cops, and there's not a thing we can do about it. She'll give the cops the run-around, tell lies, make things as difficult as she can.'

'She's crazy,' I growled.

'She's just naturally obstinate,' he corrected. 'But it's like I say, we *can't* break her, but we *can* humour her. I can give her protection, because I've got the dough. I'll employ an army of private eyes to watch over her. She won't have to know about them. I'll have experienced men on her tail day and night, watching every move she makes, watching for the guy who's trying to kill her.

'That might satisfy you,' I said bitterly. 'But it doesn't satisfy me. They've gotta wait till the killer tries again before they get a lead on him. I don't want he should even try again. Next time he might be lucky.'

Suddenly I realized I was desperately worried about Beryl, that despite her temper, her obstinacy and her contemptuous pride, there was something about her that I found lovable. She made me feel protective and unwilling to leave her in the charge of private detectives.

'I'm worried too,' he admitted. He screwed up his forehead, bit his thumb, frowned in thought.

I watched him anxiously.

He said thoughtfully: 'If only there was some way we could get her to leave here. Persuade her to go some safe place.'

I grunted. 'This killer, whoever he his, is mean and determined. He'd follow her. He'd find out where she was.'

He was still gnawing his thumb thoughtfully. It seemed to give him inspiration. 'Listen,' he said excitedly. 'We've got all the dough we need. We can fix it with a detective agency. We can get Beryl away somewhere, plant a doll in her apartment who looks like Beryl. The doll is the decoy duck. She'll be well paid for it. She'll sit there in the apartment waiting for the killer to make another attempt. When he does, I'll have so many private dicks covering the joint that he won't get a yard before there's a dozen of them on his shoulders.'

It sounded reasonable. There were only two snags. The first was the least awkward, figuring some place to take Beryl. The second seemed impossible, getting Beryl to agree to go there.

'What's a safe place and how do you get her there?' I asked.

He was still biting his thumb. Then his thoughtful expression blended into a smile of satisfaction. 'I've got it,' he said triumphantly. 'Just the thing.'

I was beginning to like him all over again. 'I'm all ears,' I told him.

'I'll send her to Terry Colman,' he said, spreading his hands, his voice implying I should now understand everything.

I stared at him, blinked. 'Terry Colman?'

He chuckled. 'You don't know about him, of course. He's one of my oldest employees. An old fella, somewhere between seventy and eighty. He's a kinda oil prospector. First-class man, lives only for his work. Got a hermit disposition. You know how it is with the oil business, folks are always looking for a gusher. That's where Terry Colman comes in. Any time we get a hint of a new well, I pack him off into the territory, leave him with a stack of supplies, and he'll be there for months, slowly covering the territory, testing and searching for new oil seams.'

'Maybe I'm dumb,' I said. 'I still don't get it.'

'Listen,' he explained. 'America's a mighty big country. Even today, with a two hundred million population, there's still whole tracts of territory that haven't been prospected. Terry Colman has just returned from a nine-months' prospecting trip. We got some crazy tip about oil in Oklahoma. It was a stretch of land, mostly desert, partly rock and mountains. We flew Terry Colman out there with enough food supplies and equipment to last three years. He was there nine months, prospected every inch of the territory before he gave up.'

'I still don't get it.'

'It's a natural,' he said excitedly. 'Terry Colman is back

now. But Beryl doesn't know that. It's miles away from anywhere, just his shack, a few stores and the nearest town sixty miles away with no road leading to it and no means of transport except walking.'

I stared at him. 'What on earth makes you think Beryl will go *there*.'

'It's a natural, like I said,' he told me with satisfaction. 'All I've got to do is say Terry's short of supplies and I've got to fly in some more. Beryl will be clamouring to make the trip for me.'

It sounded a crazy scheme. There was everything wrong with it. 'How long will it take her to fly there?'

He shrugged. 'I don't know. Maybe five or six hours.'

'The way she flies,' I told him, 'she'll be back the same day she started.'

He nodded in agreement, grinned across the table at me, tapped me on the chest with his forefinger. 'That's where you come in!'

I stared blankly. 'Me!'

'Yeah, that's our smart angle. You go with her. You'll have to make sure that for some reason or other she doesn't come back. You'll keep her there, keep her there until we've got our hands on this killer. Then I'll send for you both.'

'Now wait a minute,' I said quickly. 'I'm a reporter. I've got my work. I can't just go off like that without telling anyone, not even knowing when I'm coming back.'

'Can you suggest anyone else who will do it?' he asked.

I thought it over. There wasn't anyone I wanted to suggest. I was suspicious of everyone where Beryl was concerned.

'You know how obstinate she is,' he persuaded. 'She's gonna run herself right into real trouble. If you don't help now you've got the chance, maybe you'll spend your life regretting it.'

The idea had seemed ridiculous at first. Now it was beginning to take root in my mind and grow. It wouldn't be a tragedy to be isolated with Beryl away from everyone for a week or so. I knew she possessed some very good reasons why close confinement with her should be the opposite of a hardship.

'Okay,' I agreed reluctantly. 'Suppose I manage to get time off. Why should she take me along with her?'

'Give me your telephone number,' he said.

I gave him my card. He pocketed it carefully. 'It's like I told you, son,' he chuckled. 'You can't drive Beryl. You can only guide her. You go ahead and make your excuses to your chief. You'll learn how right I am. Tomorrow morning, she'll be on the phone asking you to go with her. I'll fix it.'

'What about Beryl tonight?'

He got up from the table. 'You sit tight while I go whip up a detective agency, get a dozen private eyes taking care of her for tonight.'

I sat back in my chair, lit another cigarette. The more I thought about this, the more I liked it. Maybe Charlie had interrupted us at a critical moment this evening.

But it looked like Charlie was making up for it, dropping a whole load of new opportunities right bang in our laps.

10

Charlie was as good as his word. The following morning, I'd no sooner fixed it with the chief and got back to my desk than she was on the phone.

'How are you fixed for getting time off?' she demanded.

'Well,' I doubted. 'I mean ... how long? What's it all about?'

'Just today, Bighead,' she snapped. 'I wanna fly the pants off you.'

'I guess maybe I can manage something,' I said doubtfully.

'Good,' she said crisply. 'Meet me at the flying field in a coupla hours.'

'I'll see if I can make it.'

'You be there,' she ordered, and hung up.

She was waiting for me when I reached the Flying Club. Charlie was there too. They were sitting at the bar, watching her plane being loaded.

I shook hands with Charlie, raised one eyebrow at Beryl. 'What goes on?' I demanded. 'Where are we going?'

'Just a little trip to see an old friend of mine,' she said offhandedly. 'What poison do you drink this time of day, beer or Scotch?'

She caught the bartender's eye, gave him my order. Charlie mystified me by saying. 'D'you feel strong, fella? How are your muscles?'

'My muscles are okay,' I said gruffly.

Beryl chuckled as Charlie shrugged wryly, took out his

wallet and found a ten-dollar note which he passed to Beryl. She tucked it away casually in the pocket of her jeans, eyed me with amused tolerance.

'What goes on?' I demanded, nettled by all this.

'A private joke between me and Beryl,' he said suavely. 'Don't let it worry you.'

I glowered, sipped my drink. The last crate of stores was being stowed in the plane. 'Okay,' said Beryl. 'Let's go.'

We walked out across the tarmac, and the cold wind tore at my trousers, seemed to cut through them and bite into my flesh. With an experienced eye, Beryl scrutinized the crates, nodded approvingly. 'Them fellas have loaded it right this time. Most times, they load it like they expect you to fly on your tail.'

Charlie said. 'Don't forget I'm expecting you back for dinner.'

'Don't you worry about me,' she told him. She gave him a playful little squeeze, rubbed her cheek against his. Then she went around the other side of the plane, climbed into the cockpit.

Charlie looked at me meaningfully, squeezed my hand with a special significance as we shook hands. 'Have a good trip, son,' he said. 'Do the best you can.'

It was a small plane, the cockpit just wide enough for two of us side by side, and the fuselage just large enough to store a fair quantity of cargo.

I climbed in beside Beryl, pulled down the unbreakable glass canopy over us so we were completely enclosed. Charlie stood back, waved his hand to us.

'You ever do any flying?' she asked as she pushed buttons, turned knobs.

'Flown a bit, one way and another,' I told her.

'Take over,' she invited. 'Let's see your form.'

I flushed. 'I've flown,' I admitted humbly, 'but I haven't piloted.'

She flashed me a look of withering contempt. 'A baby can be a passenger,' she sneered. 'But you couldn't say it had flown.'

'Okay, okay,' I said hoarsely. 'So I haven't flown.'

'You haven't lived yet, brother,' she said, and pulled another knob, which caused the engine to cough, the propeller to turn lazily.

The engine caught the fifth time she pressed the starter, and then the propeller was revolving itself into a circular, blurred haze. Then, as the motor began to warm up, the whole plane vibrated.

White-overalled grease monkeys caught Beryl's signal, ducked under the wings and pulled the chocks away from the wheels. Beryl released the brakes and the plane began to taxi, turned on to the runway, ran to the end of the field, where Beryl turned once again, thrust her foot hard down on the throttle to race the engine.

'All set?' she shouted above the roar of the engine.

I settled myself more firmly in the seat. 'All set,' I shouted back grimly. Now I was actually sitting in the plane beside her, all kinds of doubts were assailing me. She might decide to try that head-on dive at the club-house again, just to impress me. This time, with a load of weighty stores packed in the fuselage behind us, the plane might not reply promptly enough.

I began to sweat.

'Here we go,' she shouted, and in that moment she looked so adorable with her shining eyes and keen, eager face that I wanted to wrap my arms around her.

She could fly. Flying musta been in her blood, musta been part of her life. I never knew the exact moment the wheels left the ground, only became suddenly conscious that the earth was sliding down away from us at a sharp angle, the club-house, the trees and the car park rapidly becoming smaller while the horizon unrolled itself, revealing an intricate pattern of fields and roads that diminished swiftly to map-like proportions.

She circled, dropped the nose of the plane and levelled off in a dead-straight line before she relaxed. 'Gimme a cigarette, Bighead,' she invited.

I gave her a cigarette, lit one myself. I'd always understood it was dangerous to smoke in a plane. But my pride wouldn't allow me to point it out. It wouldn't have made any difference anyway. She'd have scoffed at me.

'Where are we going?' I asked.

She grinned impudently. 'Delivering groceries,' she chuckled.

'Why do I have to come along?' I had to back up Charlie, keep the pretence going.

'You'll help with the unloading,' she told me sweetly.

I glared. 'What's that I'm supposed to do?'

She thumbed over her shoulder. 'Terry Colman's an old guy. He's smart, but he's not strong. Not very strong. I need a tough guy to unload those stores from the plane.'

My face reddened. 'Is this supposed to be funny?' I asked nastily. 'Manoeuvring me on a trip just so I can unload?'

Her hazel eyes were dancing. 'There's more to it than that,' she said. 'I won ten dollars too. Charlie bet me I couldn't get you along on this trip.'

I understood why Charlie had done this, but it didn't make me feel any the more comfortable. I settled back in my seat, shrouded myself in a ruffled, angry silence.

'Cut it out, Bighead,' she said, grinning.

I glared at her.

'Surely you can take a little ribbing.'

I glared some more.

She leaned over until her shoulder touched mine, tilted her head around to stare up into my face with a winning smile. 'Come on, grumpy,' she chided. 'Don't be sulky. Let's see you give me a nice big smile.'

Her nearness was pleasant, her persuasion intoxicating. My own lips twitched despite themselves, and then suddenly I was smiling too.

'That's my boy,' she said.

I chuckled.

She chuckled.

My chuckle became a hearty laugh. She stopped chuckling, eyed me suspiciously. 'What's so funny?' she demanded.

I could have told her, but I didn't. I could have told her that as soon as I touched down, I was gonna take my revenge in full.

Instead I said: 'It's kinda funny the way you pulled a fast one on me. Me walking into it like a simpleton.'

'Bighead!' she chuckled.

We covered a lotta territory. Half-an-hour after we left Chicago, we ran into clouds. She climbed above them, flew on instruments across a thick, white sea of cotton wool, through which we caught an occasional glimpse of the brown earth below.

Three and a half hours after leaving Chicago, we put down at a small airstrip, stayed long enough to refuel our tanks.

The last stage of the journey was absorbing. We left the green fields and farmland behind us, passed over mountain ranges, noticed that the towns were further and further apart. Finally we came to rough, rugged, semi-mountainous country, thickly wooded and a danger to pilots having to make a forced landing. This rugged territory slowly blended into scrubland; dry, unfertile ground that was barren, inhospitable and devoid of habitation.

We completed the journey in just five hours, and a more godforsaken spot I've never seen.

She circled the place twice so I could get a good look at the surrounding countryside. If you could call it countryside, that is.

It was a kinda small oval of raised hillocks set down in a wilderness of desert and rocks. In the centre of the oval was a natural plateau, which formed a ready-made airstrip. At the far end of the plateau was a tiny, roughly-built wooden shack, which Beryl indicated. 'Terry Colman must be asleep,' she said. 'He'd have been out by now to wave us in.'

'Do we need his help?' I asked anxiously.

She looked at me pityingly. 'What do you think?' she mocked, and put the plane into a steep bank that caused me to lie on my side.

She didn't try any tricks, took a long run in, landed as gently as a feather and taxied to the far end of the narrow plateau where the shack stood.

'Well, that's it,' she sighed with relief. Her fingers were busy, switching off the engine, touching this contact, severing that connection. I was closely watching all her actions.

'The canopy, Bighead,' she said. 'Open the canopy.'

I slid it back, and with athletic grace she swung herself from the cockpit, dropped neatly to the ground.

I hadn't spent five hours in that plane without examining the instrument board carefully. I opened the instrument panel at the side, reached in behind the dials, grabbed a handful of wires at random and ripped them away from their connections.

She was striding over towards the shack, her whole attitude expressing surprise at not seeing Terry Colman.

She was a smart dame. She probably knew as much about aero engines as she did about car engines. Swiftly I twisted the loose ends of the wires together, making new contacts and hoping like hell they would cause a blowout. Then, as she pushed open the door of the shack, I reached for the tap that jettisoned petrol when the plane was in difficulties. I switched it on and jumped hurriedly from the plane, walked quickly to the shack.

I met her in the doorway as she came out, eyes wide with surprise and indignation. 'There's no-one here,' she said. 'What the hell's been happening? Looks like the place has been cleaned out.'

I took her by the shoulder, bundled her inside again. I shut the door behind me, got my shoulders against it without deliberately seeming to do so. I stared around the shack stupidly. 'Looks like it's empty,' I said.

'Of course it's empty,' she snarled.

'What does it mean?' I asked blankly. 'Do we still unload the stores?'

'It means Charlie's got it all wrong,' she said in annoyance. 'There's no equipment here, no stores, nothing. So Terry must have packed up for good.'

'Well, let's have a cigarette and then fly back,' I said pacifically.

She cocked her head on one side. 'Can you hear water running?'

I listened. I could hear the petrol splashing on to the soaked earth beneath the fuselage. I said, with a perplexed tone in my voice: 'Water running?'

'Sure,' she said. 'Water.' She listened some more, then pushed me away from the door. Or tried to.

'Take it easy, lady,' I said. 'Who are you pushing around?'

'Don't be a fool, Bighead,' she said irritably. She thrust at me, was surprised when I used my weight, stood stolidly braced against the door.

'You're getting foolish, Beryl,' I said. 'You can't hear water running.'

Her hazel eyes glared into mine. Perhaps woman's intuition came to her aid. I saw her eyes widen, then flame with anger. Her jaw jutted as she went into startlingly dynamic action.

It wasn't her fist against my jaw that hurt. It was the unexpected, agonizing, driving jag of her knee in the pit of my belly. I grunted as air whooshed out from my lungs. I plunged sideways, doubled up as numbing agony paralysed me from the waist down.

I was on my knees, agony clutching at my belly and dragging me down into the earth while a grey blur shimmered before my eyes. Yet I had to stop her. For her own sake I had to stop her.

I shook the sweat drops from my forehead, braced myself against the wall of the shack, strained to my feet with shafts of red hot pain stabbing through to my backbone. The sweat was running into my eyes as I got the door open, propped myself in the doorway, saw her clambering into the cockpit. I took a coupla unsteady, shaky paces towards her and couldn't make it, dropped on my knees, stared impotently as the white jet of escaping petrol eased to a trickle then ceased altogether as she turned off the cock.

I didn't know how much petrol had been lost. But she had all the gauges in front of her. She could tell if she had enough to get some place to refuel. She figured she had. She pressed the starter, the engine coughed, coughed a second time, coughed a third time.

The fourth time it didn't cough; there was a kinda flash, and a cloud of blue smoke burst out from behind the propeller shaft, ballooned upwards.

She was a smart kid. She knew all about aeroplanes and fires. She was out of that plane quicker than a flash, stood watching it from twenty yards as the dwindling blue smoke spiralled away into nothingness.

There was nothing more I needed to do. Short-circuiting leads had done it all for me. I got to my feet weakly, leaned against the shack while she returned to the plane, searched and examined.

It was hot there. I hadn't noticed it previously, being in the upper rarefied air. But on the ground, the sun was bouncing off the dry earth, billowing upwards like a thick, invisible blanket. I could feel sweat trickling down between my shoulder blades, my underclothing damp and sticking to me. I was beginning to get my breath back too, the pain in my belly easing to a dull ache.

However much an engineer she may have been, her face as she clambered out of the cockpit told me the repairs were beyond her ability. And as she strode across to me with eyes flaming and determination and anger in every line of her slim, young body, I felt an irresistible impulse to rush inside the shack, shut the door and protect myself from her anger.

I didn't do it. I stood my ground, leaning against the shack, still feeling sick and weak.

She came right up to me, stood with legs astride, hands on hips and eyes flaming into mine. 'You did it,' she accused. 'You crossed those leads and jettisoned the petrol.' She was breathless with anger.

I didn't say anything. I licked my lips.

'My plane,' she burst out, almost crying with anger. 'You almost ruined my plane, almost burnt it out.' She swept forward and her palm cracked against my cheek, her other hand swung, smashed my head back against the hard wood of the cabin.

I took it. I still felt sick from the pain in my guts, but I stood there and took it.

'You imbecile,' she mouthed. 'You dirty, sneaking, lying swine. It mighta gone up in flames. My plane! You coulda destroyed it completely.' She threw herself at me in her rage, pounded my chest with her fists, smashed her knuckles into my face.

I stood braced against the cabin, feeling sick and making no attempt to defend myself. So sick, I hardly noticed the pain of her fists. She exhausted her fury, stepped back, eyed me furiously, breasts heaving as she panted.

I braced myself against the cabin, eyed her steadily. Her voice rose to an hysterical scream. 'Why d'you do it?'

I raised the back of my hand to the corner of my mouth, wiped away blood, eyed her steadily and still said nothing.

'Why d'you do it?' she demanded, and this time her voice was almost a whisper.

I felt sick. Jeepers I felt sick. Her knee had jagged so deep into my belly it had bruised my spine. I felt weak and faint and the sun was getting me, too. I pressed my shoulders against the wall, still said nothing.

Now there was understanding in her eyes. 'You fixed this,' she accused. 'You and Charlie fixed it between you. That's what happened. You planned to get me here and keep me here.'

I didn't wanna do it, but I couldn't fight it any longer. My knees buckled and I slid down the wall into a sitting position.

She stared at me for a long while. Her beautiful face expressed a riot of conflicting emotions: anger, suspicion, anxiousness, concern and worry. She said irritably: 'You're as white as a sheet. D'you feel ill or something?'

'No,' I gritted. 'I kick myself there for fun ten times a day. I'm used to it.'

She was worried but wouldn't show it. 'You asked for it,' she defended.

'I'm not complaining,' I grunted, sweating. It was easier sitting down. It relieved the strain on my stomach muscles.

She stared for a long while, kinda waging an internal fight. 'Listen, Bighead,' she said grudgingly. 'Is there anything I can do?'

I was getting over it now. I could feel my strength coming back to me. It musta been the sun and the numbing pain combined that had made me suddenly weak. But this was just too good an opportunity to pass up. I allowed a groan of pain to escape my lips, allowed my head to drop limply on one side. 'Nothing,' I said weakly. 'Maybe a doctor, but that's impossible ...' My voice trailed on.

She was down on her knees beside me now, hands supporting my head, worried eyes staring anxiously into mine. 'What is it, Hank?' she breathed. 'Where does it hurt you most? What can I do about it?'

'Nothing .. can ... do,' I muttered feebly. 'All ... twisted up ... inside!'

She cushioned my cheek against her breasts, wrapped her arms around me, held me tightly, kinda sobbing with worry and concern. 'I didn't mean it, darling. I'll do anything. Anything. Tell me what I can do. I didn't know ... I didn't mean ... I wasn't thinking!'

'Just hold me tightly,' I whispered faintly, my eyes closed, her nearness intoxicating.

Her soft fingers brushed the hair from my forehead, and the worry in her voice was sharp and urgent as she blamed herself. 'Believe me. Darling. I didn't know what I was doing. It's my dreadful temper. I've done this to you while you were only wanting to help me. You did it for me, didn't you, darling? You wanted to keep me away from danger. Darling, tell me what I can do. I must be able to do something.'

The closeness of her, the softness of her was too much for me. My arms slipped around her, held her tightly and intimately. I'd have liked to have continued my pretending, but my emotions had got the better of me.

Her emotions were working overtime too. It was maybe two or three minutes before she realized my grip and ambitions were those of a healthy man.

She struggled, pushed herself away from me vigorously, glared into my laughing face. 'You were acting,' she accused indignantly. 'You're not hurt at all.'

'You want I should be hurt?' I asked, chuckling.

I should have remembered her palm. It really stung this time. While my tongue was exploring my mouth, wondering how many loose teeth it would encounter, she got to her feet, stalked over to a rock embedded in the earth, sat on it and glared at me furiously as she lit a cigarette.

I got to my feet slowly, grinned across at her. 'Wanna get sunstroke?'

'Keep outta my way,' she said in an ugly voice. 'Keep well away from me. If you come near, don't blame me for what happens. The next time, you won't get any sympathy. You'll die for all I care.'

'Looks like we're gonna be here quite a time,' I said conversationally. 'It might be difficult keeping up this unsocial act.'

She got up abruptly, walked across to the plane, climbed up into the cockpit. She came back with something that glinted in the sun. She levelled it at me. 'I'll make this my argument,' she said grimly. 'Keep away from me or I'll use it.'

I chuckled meekly. 'Okay, honey,' I said. 'Have it your way.' I pushed through the door of the shack and sat comfortably in the doorway where I was in the shade and protected from the searing rays of the hot sun.

It was an ideal vantage point from which to watch her as she sat on the dry, hot earth, staring at me malevolently.

I fumbled cigarettes from my pack, lit up happily. I was certain she'd have to get sociable sooner or later, share the shack with me, or be sun scorched.

11

Did I say it was a godforsaken hole?

It was sixty miles to the nearest town. The sun was beating down on the small, wooden shack and the dry sandy earth was shimmering in the heat. Just by the door of the shack was a metal trough containing a thick, glossy black substance that looked and smelt like a mixture of oil and tar. It was all that was left of Terry Colman's oil prospecting.

It was so hot I'd stripped to the waist now, was sweating from every pore, and had an unholy thirst.

Thirst!

WATER!

I went over to the plane with a quick half-run, half-shuffle. Beryl must have been baking. But obstinately she sat there fully exposed to the sun, watching me balefully with angry, glinting eyes.

Pulling out those crates and tumbling them on the ground made me sweat twice as much, made me four times as thirsty.

There was canned meat, coffee, canned condensed milk, canned beans and tobacco. I was getting anxious, desperately anxious. I pulled out the last crate and found it was canned pineapple juice. But it was such a small crate, containing so few tins.

I straightened up, walked across to Beryl. She got up quickly, pointed the revolver at my belly. 'Keep away from me,' she snarled. 'I've warned you. Don't drive me to it.'

'We're in a jam. You've got to know where we stand,' I said. 'We've got maybe a dozen tins of pineapple juice to drink. That and nothing more.'

Her lips curled contemptuously. 'Use your brains, Bighead,' she rasped. 'Don't you know the plane's fitted with a water tank?'

I turned away from her, ran back to the plane. I found the tank at the back of the fuselage, complete with water cock. I turned the tap, and it was like music as water splashed on the floor of the fuselage. I switched off quickly. Water was precious here, far too precious to be squandered.

I opened up a tin of pineapple juice, quenched my thirst. There was still half the tin left. I took it over to Beryl, stopped a couple of yards from her, put it on the ground. 'That's for when you get thirsty,' I told her.

She didn't say anything, just stared at me with those glinting eyes. She made no attempt to touch the tin.

I left her alone with her obstinacy. She'd have to break sooner or later. I didn't have to do anything. Nature would do all that was necessary. I began transferring the stores from the plane to the shack. The sun was beating down and I took it very steadily. When I was through, I sat down in the shade of the shack, lit a cigarette.

I was wrong about nature causing her to break. The hot sun and thirst was only a challenge to her.

She got to her feet, walked over to me, still holding that revolver pointing at my belly. She rasped in a hard voice: 'How far to the nearest town?'

I grinned. 'About sixty miles,' I said cheerfully.

'That's just too bad for you,' she said with narrowed eyes.

'Is zat so?' I grinned.

'Zat's so,' she mocked. 'Because we're gonna start walking right now, and since you're the one who's made it necessary, you can do the humping. We'll need water, and we'll need food. So get busy, make yourself a comfortable haversack while you're about it because you're sure gonna feel tired by the time we get through.'

I grinned at her impudently. 'You oughta come in the shade,' I said. 'The sun's got you sooner than I expected.'

'On your feet,' she said coldly.

'Settle down, lady,' I advised 'Get wise to yourself. We're here for a long time. We're here till that killer's rounded up. So settle down, take things easy.'

'Get up,' she rasped.

'You're wasting your time,' I said. 'Go bowl a hoop.'

She put a bullet through the shack door, not three inches from my ear. The crack of the revolver and the smack of the bullet ploughing through wood was simultaneous.

Now I'm not a jumpy guy. But I'm human. And I figure any guy who has lead ploughed into wood a few inches from his head is gonna find it shocks him right down his spine. It certainly shocked me. She'd fired at point-blank range. The blast of the gun twanged my nerve strings, the smack of the bullet turned my bones to jelly. In startled fright I said inanely, 'Hey!'

'On your feet,' she rasped. 'Or maybe you want your ears shot off.'

I didn't want my ears shot off. The blood was running to my head, boiling into a red mist. I wanted to get my hands on her, slap that rounded rear of hers until she howled for mercy.

I got up like an infuriated Goliath, angered by fright, burning with resentment and reaction from shock.

Maybe she thought she'd scared me into submission or maybe she'd have fired anyway if she'd have got the chance. I don't know. I got to my feet and dived at her almost in the same movement. My outstretched fingers clutched her gun wrist as my shoulder smashed into her thigh.

We hit the ground together, she underneath and the gun slithering across the ground yards away. She wriggled like an eel, jabbed with her knee, bit the back of my neck with firm, white teeth.

I wasn't worried about her. I was worried about the gun. Once I got my hands on that, it eliminated the only danger she could confront me with. I was confident I could handle her without that.

I got to the gun while she was still scrambling to her feet. I thrust it deep into my trousers pocket, then turned quickly to meet her savage rush.

I was still angry, still smarting from the shock of fright the bullet had given me. I caught her round the waist, twisted her around, half-bent her over my knee and got in one good slap on tightly-stretched material before her heel uppercutted me beneath the chin.

I sat down hard, shook my head, trying not to see stars. Then the weight of her bore me backwards and she was straddled astride my chest, hands grasping my hair, hammering my head like she was gonna dig a hole in the ground with it while angry eyes flamed into mine.

A guy can take just so much of that treatment. I almost forgot she was a dame, rolled her off my chest, punched at her chin, remembering only in the last moment that she wasn't a man. I just failed to pull my punch.

As a sock on the chin it was a joke, a gentle punch of affection. But the jolt it gave to her feminine pride was tremendous.

To be punched on the chin! To be hit by a man!

She hadn't been angry before. She'd been a tame, playful kitten compared with the enraged tigress she now became.

How do you cope with a wildcat anyway? With a guy it's simple. You sock him and he socks you until one of you is too exhausted to go on punching.

With a dame it's different. You can't sock them. Meanwhile, they're busy using nails, teeth, fists and feet on you. I didn't want to hurt her. I was supposed to be looking after her. I twisted away from her, ran towards the door of the shack which was welcomingly and protectively open. Her long nails had ripped skin from my left cheek, my shins ached from the impact of toe caps, my wrists were bleeding where sharp teeth had almost bitten out chunks of flesh, and hard knuckles had pummelled my ribs.

She was quicker than I believed possible, intercepted me, got between me and the doorway with claws upraised to slash, face red with anger.

I came to an abrupt stop, eyed her cautiously.

She moved in on me slowly.

I raised one hand half defensively, half soothingly. 'Now don't let's get excited, honey,' I began.

She put her head down and charged straight at me. She musta had some idea about smacking me in the bread basket with her head, knocking me off my feet and trampling on me. But if she'd been a guy instead of a dame, she'd have learned long ago it's fatal to go in with your head down.

I waited until the last moment before I dodged to one side. I was well balanced, beautifully poised. I did it almost with the grace of a bullfighter. As she blundered past, my waiting upraised palm followed through with a hard slap on her pants that rang out on the hot air with the sharpness of a pistol shot. It increased the speed of her charge by at least fifty per cent.

I'd forgotten the trough of black, oily mixture. I was standing right in front of it when she rushed me. I didn't remember it until I saw her hurtling towards it, stumbling, arms waving as she vainly tried to regain her balance.

She hit the trough, half sprawled over it. It wouldn't have been so bad if the trough had remained firmly rooted in the ground. But it toppled over, sprawling her on the dry earth in a wide pool of thick, glutinous, treacly blackness.

She gave a howl, hastily scrambled to her feet, slipped and sat down squarely in the awful mixture.

It musta been hot through simmering in that hot sun. She tried to wrench herself free and it clung to her grimly like black treacle, thick and evil-smelling now it had been stirred up.

Her blue jeans were smothered in it, her windjammer and sweater thick with it. Only her hair and her face escaped soiling. I stood and watched with growing horror as in her fierce efforts to extricate herself she slipped, fell again, wallowed in that awful, black mess, howling all the time with horror and anger.

She got to her knees, climbed carefully to her feet.

Just in time, the 'love-of-life' spirit that dwells inside all of us, the will to self-preservation that we all have, came to my rescue, yelled lustily into my consciousness.

'Listen, dope,' it hollered. 'She's hopping mad. Scram. Scram, you dope, before she gets her hands on you.'

It was good sound sense. She'd been difficult to handle before. Now, enveloped in that tar-like concoction, she'd be ten times more unpleasant to handle.

I turned on my heel, raced for the plane. I climbed up into the cockpit, pulled down the glass canopy and fastened it firmly from the inside.

It took her a few more minutes to completely extricate herself. Then, with some kinda dumb, dim idea of cleaning herself, she rolled on the sandy, dusty ground.

It didn't help much. Merely converted her into a kinda bundle of walking roof-felting. And that was when she hit the zenith of her anger.

She'd have killed me if she could have got at me. She used rocks to try and smash in the canopy, hurled abuse at me, thrust and shoved at the plane like she wanted to overturn it. At one time, I was scared she'd go completely crazy and set the plane on fire with me in it.

Then inevitably as her anger cooled she became conscious of something else. That tar-like, messy substance had coated her clothing her from head to toe. It was taking time, but slowly was penetrating her clothing. The thought of that gooey, evil-smelling stickiness actually touching her flesh musta been revolting.

I didn't get it at first, stared in astonishment as she ripped off her windjammer, carefully coaxed her sweater over her hair and then stripped off shoes, socks and jeans.

I did understand, however, when she began to spread her clothing in the sun with the forlorn hope it would dry out. And by that time, I was far too interested watching Beryl to worry about the reasons she was this way.

I suppose there are bikini bathing suits that would have shown more of her than did her scanty briefs and brassiere. But somehow this was kinda special, me being the only admirer on the beach as it were.

I propped open the glass canopy so I could see even more clearly.

Yeah, those briefs were scanty. Fine like silk, and tight.

As she bent over, spreading out her clothing, they stretched tautly, showing ...

As though she could feel my eyes she, spun around suddenly, flashed me a look of disgust, reached for a handy rock and slung it with such accuracy and force that if I hadn't got the canopy closed quickly, it would have been embedded in my forehead.

I turned my attention to her brassiere. It was well-tailored, well-shaped. It had plenty of uplift and out-thrust to cope with, and wasn't entirely adequate for its job. I pointed, grinned with pleasure, raised one thumb and winked to show my approval.

Her furious face glared. Then her eyes switched from me to where I was looking. She flashed me another withering look, clasped her hands across her breasts, tossed her head in outraged indignation and ran towards the shack.

I lit myself another cigarette, smiled with satisfaction. It was a tough party, but it looked like having its advantages. It didn't look to me like Beryl was ever gonna wear those clothes again. And since we were probably gonna be together alone for a long while, I wasn't gonna find it a hardship having her around dressed just the way she was. Then my jaw dropped. I glared with disappointment as she reappeared in the doorway of the shack.

I shouldn't have been so careless. I shouldn't have left them lying around that way. Because my shirt draped around her waist was a reasonable substitute for a skirt, and my jacket, although several sizes too large, was fulfilling the ignoble task of concealing all the brassiere didn't.

She stood in the doorway of the shack, and stared at me triumphantly.

I glared back.

Then, with a completely unladylike gesture, yet somehow with queenly dignity, she put her tongue out at me.

12

She was the one who had the shade now, and I was stuck up there in the cockpit of the plane while the sun beat down on the glass canopy, turning the interior into an oven and me into a roast.

But the sun was my comrade as well as my enemy. Even Beryl couldn't go on being mad all the time, with the heat burning the energy out of her and sapping her strength. I raised the canopy and let out some of the hot, stuffy air that was slowly baking me. She sat within the shade of the shack watching me, made no further attempts to smash my head with rocks. I pushed the canopy all the way open, watched her cautiously. She sat there in the shade of the shack, arms resting on her knees, chin resting on her arms. The shack was preventing the direct rays of the sun from hitting her, but it musta been plenty hot inside.

And it was plenty hot inside the plane, too. The metalwork around the cockpit was almost red hot, blistering to the touch. I remembered the water, crawled back into the fuselage, moistened my lips.

She musta been thirsty too. I stuck my head through the canopy, called over to her. 'Feeling thirsty?'

'What's it to you?' she called back.

The hot sun was like a thousand red-hot needles probing my bare chest and shoulders. I was ready to compromise if she was.

'Don't let's keep this up,' I pleaded. 'There's water up here. You must be dying of thirst. What say we call a truce?'

She thought it over. 'I'm promising nothing,' she warned.

'Will you quit wild-catting for ten minutes?' I asked.

She took a long while to think that over. 'I guess so,' she agreed dully.

That was good enough for me. I climbed out of the plane, finished off the pineapple juice in the half-empty tin she'd refused to touch. It was as warm as tea. I used the tin as a container for water, half-filled it and took it over to her.

She sipped at it gratefully as I sat down beside her. Yeah, it sure was hot in that shack. The air was heavy, roasted, difficult to breathe. And wearing my jacket merely for the sake of modesty was too high a price to pay. She let it slip off her shoulders. Close up, I could see just how amply filled that tight brassiere was.

'Give me a cigarette,' she ordered.

I lit it for her, noticed her damp cheeks, the perspiration gleaming on her bare shoulders, the glistening beads that trembled and shimmered, slipped out of sight down the valley between her breasts.

'It was a crazy thing to do,' she said in a fed-up voice. 'We're stuck here miles from anywhere, no means of transport and being reduced to grease spots.'

'I had to do it, honey,' I told her. 'You just won't take care of yourself. Somebody's got to do it for you.'

'Just how do we get out of here, anyway?'

'It's all fixed,' I told her. 'Charlie's got a squad of private dicks watching your apartment. He's even hired a dame who looks like you, to be a sitting duck. Sooner or later that killer's gonna have another crack at you. Or rather at the substitute. The next time he won't get away with it.'

'You fixed it with Charlie?' she said breathlessly.

'He's worried about you too, honey.'

'And how do we get out of here?'

'As soon as the killer's safely under lock and key, Charlie's gonna send for us.'

'I think it was mean of both of you,' she said. 'You could at least have discussed it with me.'

'Would you have listened?'

She changed her position, kinda half lay on the floor of the shack, supporting her weight on her elbows. 'I guess not,' she admitted.

'Well now you're here, be sensible about it,' I pleaded. 'It couldn't have been pleasant knowing someone was perpetually trying to get you free transport to the morgue. Why not accept things as they are?'

She sighed. 'I guess I've got no choice.'

We sat there in silence for a while, me watching her hot, moist skin, while she pretended she didn't know I was watching.

'I'll go crazy waiting here,' she said irritably. 'Just sitting here waiting with nothing to do, being burnt alive all the time.'

'Time'll go quickly enough,' I reassured her. 'Get busy, do something. When you're working, time passes more quickly.'

Her lips twisted in a sneer. 'Just what does one do here?'

'Feeling hungry?'

She looked at me from the corner of her eye. 'You suggesting I should cook?'

'Not cook,' I corrected. 'Just rustle up something cold.'

There was a long silence. Her hazel eyes were looking deep into mine, examining my face, trying to probe my thoughts. 'I bet you've forgotten the tin opener,' she said at last.

'We don't need a tin opener. I've got a boy scout's knife: cuts string, takes stones out of horses' hooves and opens tins.'

'Let me have it,' she grinned, suddenly sociable. 'I guess I'm as good a cook with a tin-opener as the next girl.'

The sun set with unexpected swiftness, and presented us with the problem of light. The answer was simple. I built a fire from the broken stores crates. But it only solved the problem for that night. The following night, when no more stores crates were left, unless we systematically began to take the shack to pieces, we'd have no light.

The fire helped with another problem too. The problem of warmth.

That may sound funny. But as soon as that sun set, the cold began to hit us. The contrast between the heat of the day and the cold of the night was tremendous. We crouched around the fire, kept as close to it as we could, Beryl with my jacket around her shoulders and me with my shirt over my sun-scorched shoulders.

Then, as our supply of firewood grew lower, so it became colder, the night wind blowing up, cutting across the hard earth, stinging our faces with grit, causing us to shiver uncontrollably.

We tried sheltering from it in the shack; discovered cutting draughts whistling through the wide cracks in the sun-dried wood.

'I'm freezing, Hank,' she told me, teeth chattering.

'What about your clothes?'

'Ugh.' She shivered involuntarily. 'Hopeless. An oily, sticky mess. Doubt if I could get in them.'

'There's only one other thing for it,' I told her. 'We'll spend the night in the plane. It'll be uncomfortable, but tomorrow we'll get busy, look around and find dead wood so we can build a fire that'll last all night.'

'I can stand anything, provided I'm warm,' she said, shivering.

We climbed into the plane, sat side by side like we would in a car, pulled the canopy down over us. It cut off the wind, left the two of us alone, enclosed in a small private world that was peculiarly ours.

'How's that?' I asked.

'Better. But I'm still cold.'

'You want I should put my arm around you, help you get warm?'

'You're quick off the mark,' she told me. 'I was calculating how long we'd be here before you did that.'

'Listen,' I said angrily. 'For all I care, you can freeze to death. But I'm not all that warm myself. I was merely making a suggestion that would benefit both of us and ...'

'Sure, sure,' she chuckled. 'But get started, will ya? Don't talk yourself into freezing both of us.'

She may have been cold, but she didn't feel cold to me. Not when my arm was around her and she was snuggled up to me with her cheek resting on my shoulder. We shared my jacket between us, draped it around the front of us. And because her legs were cold, I stripped off my shirt, draped it around her waist.

With the canopy closed, it was surprising how quickly it warmed up in there. Within half-an-hour we were both as warm as toast. And that wasn't merely on account the cockpit was warm. Because by then we weren't only warmed up, we were steamed up!

She said huskily: 'Kinda funny, ain't it, Hank? All those opportunities back in town where I had a comfortable flat, and yet we haven't really got together until we're in a damned uncomfortable and cramped position.'

It *was* uncomfortable. Damned uncomfortable. Yet it was delightful too; exhilaratingly delightful. I knew all that a bead of sweat could know and much more. And despite her tough, hard exterior and attitude, in a clinch Beryl was as feminine as they're made, as kittenish and as playful as any guy could want, provided it didn't drive him crazy.

She whispered: 'You're cute, honey.'

'You're cute, too.'

There was a long period during which we didn't speak. She broke the silence. 'You devil, Hank,' she whispered breathlessly.

'You make me this way.'

She gave a sudden gasp, buried her face against my chest, clenched her firm white teeth into my flesh until I thrilled all over and wanted to shout aloud with the sharp, sweet pain of it.

'Hank,' she panted, and her nails were gouging into my

arms.

'Hank,' she whispered, and she was trembling all over, vibrating, so hot her skin was slippery.

'Hank,' she moaned.

'This damned thing,' I growled.

It was the joy-stick, inconveniently situated almost beneath the two bucket seats, obstructive and mocking.

'Get it out of the way,' she whispered urgently. 'Do something about it.'

'Move this way,' I directed. I showed her how.

'Hank,' she whispered. 'Damn you, Hank. I've never been this way before. Why am I crazy like this?'

'I'm crazy, too.'

'Bite my ear again, Hank, the way you did just now.'

'Like this?'

'Hank!' she whispered breathlessly. 'Hank!'

It was wildly exciting, never-endingly stimulating, pleasant and dreamlike. I didn't remember going to sleep, and she musta dozed off too with her head on my chest.

It was a loudly buzzing bee and the heat that awoke me. The bee was vibrating inside my head and the heat was burning me up, drying every drop of moisture in my body.

I opened my eyes, blinked against the white hot, dazzling sunlight. The heat swept over me in hot, suffocating waves. I reached up, opened the canopy, slid it wide open. My sudden movement wakened Beryl and increased the buzzing of the bee to the roar of aircraft.

That brought me into wakefulness with a start. I stood up in the cockpit, shaded my eyes from the fierce glare of the sun, peered into the sky.

Beryl was standing up beside me. 'He's circling,' she said excitedly. 'Maybe he's gonna land.'

'That'd be crazy,' I said. 'Why would anyone land here?'

'Maybe he was passing, saw us grounded, thought we were in trouble.'

I looked down at her. Her face was alive with hope and eagerness.

'Honey,' I said softly.

'Hank.' She slid her hand into mine, intimately and trustingly.

'If it is,' I said. 'You don't want to go back, do you? I mean, now we're here, it's best to stay. You do understand that, don't you, honey?'

She was still staring up at the aircraft, her face eager. She said, like she wasn't even listening to me: 'We'll see, Hank. We'll see.'

The plane was a small one. It made a complete circle around us, so low we could see the blur of the pilot in his cockpit. Then he skimmed away almost out of sight, before he turned around, headed straight in towards us.

'He's coming down,' she said excitedly. 'He's gonna land, Hank.'

'We'd better go and meet him,' I said gruffly. I was angry. It would be unfortunate if Charlie's plans were upset by the arrival of an unexpected rescuer.

'It's gonna be okay, Hank,' she said excitedly.

'Yeah,' I grunted, and vaulted out from the cockpit. She began to clamber out after me.

'We've got company,' I warned her.

She flushed, ducked back quickly into the cockpit. The plane was a good way off and was still coming in low down when she started to clamber out from the cockpit a second time.

'Beryl,' I said anxiously.

She hesitated, looked at me enquiringly.

'Put on the jacket as well.'

She grinned at me impudently. 'Jealous?'

'Jealous, hell,' I grunted. 'I just don't want you should catch cold.'

She chuckled, but I was relieved when she did what I asked. She even buttoned it up at the front, which was an even greater relief. If I was gonna argue a rescuing pilot into not taking us with him, it would be a disadvantage to show him good reasons for hanging around and trying to persuade us.

She clambered down from the cockpit, took my hand as the plane's wheels touched down at our end of the runway. It was a good long run in. The plane came in over the top of the shack, touched down, ran almost the full length of the runway before it came to a standstill, turned around to face us.

Beryl's forehead puckered. 'Strange,' she said. 'Wonder what he's doing here? It's a flying-school plane. One of those you hire by the hour. What the hell's he doing in this neck of the woods?'

'What the hell's he doing way up there?' I asked.

The plane wasn't taxiing down the length of the runway towards us. Instead, the pilot had turned off the engine, was sitting up there in the cockpit. It was almost as though he was waiting for us.

'Let's go,' said Beryl. She burst into a run, pulling me along behind her.

I didn't see any need to hurry. We'd get there sooner or later. I dragged along behind her, and presently the sun and my weight got her. She relaxed into a swift walk. So, hand in hand, we innocently walked towards that plane.

Maybe it was Beryl's casual remark about it being strange for a hire-by-the-hour plane to be in that remote part of the world. Maybe it was some strange sixth sense. Maybe it was just a natural suspicion.

I was uneasy.

'Why the hell do we have to walk up to him? Why can't he taxi down to us?' I grumbled.

'Maybe he's short of petrol,' she said. 'Wants to conserve it.'

We were getting near the plane now, close enough to see the leather flying helmet and goggles of the pilot as he levered himself out from the cockpit, dropped to the ground.

'See,' she said triumphantly. 'He's coming to meet us.'

She was wrong. He'd turned, was fumbling in the cockpit. As he withdrew it, the sun glinted on the long barrel, and the spark of suspicion in my mind flamed into certainty.

It was my turn to pull Beryl now, running like a crazy man

dragging her unwillingly behind me, as she yelled a protest, tugged against me, tried to pull her hand free.

She wasn't usually slow on the uptake. But she was slow now. Or maybe she hadn't seen the silvery glint of the rifle barrel, didn't realize we'd obligingly walked within range of it. I shot a quick glance over my shoulder, saw him standing there, a vague, chunky figure in flying jacket and goggles, levelling the rifle, sighting carefully.

I zig-zagged frantically, running as hard as I knew how, all the time with the dragging weight of Beryl trying to pull me to a standstill and the dreadful knowledge that we were out in the wide open, living targets.

Maybe it was the hot sun causing the ground to shimmer, perhaps my zig-zagging movement or even his own confidence. He shouldn't have done it, but he missed.

The crack of the rifle was like thunder, echoing and echoing around us, and the sudden spurt of dried earth to our left as a screaming bullet ricocheted told Beryl everything.

She flung a scared glance over her shoulder, began running as hard as me.

'Separate,' I yelled at her. 'Make for those rocks over there.'

We split up, ran with three or four yards between us, so he'd have two moving targets, instead of one grouped target. But he didn't fire again. He was too confident, figured he had everything under control.

We reached the rocks, panting with perspiration. They could hardly be called shelter. Two big, rounded rocks embedded in the hard earth on a small hillock.

We cowered down behind the rocks, drew air into our aching lungs. The rocks were white, burning to the touch. Cautiously I peered from behind mine, saw that chunky figure leisurely strolling towards us.

I realized then why he hadn't bothered to fire a second time. He had all the time in the world. He'd even taken time off to light himself a cigarette.

Yeah, he had us sewn up in a sack. Carried under his arm, like he was stalking rabbits, was a repeating rifle. With that, he could pick both of us off neatly and cleanly. It was a day's hunting for him. If we ran, he would follow. Sooner or later we'd get tired, rest, and then he'd catch up with us, pick us off carefully from a distance. And if we didn't run, waited for him instead, he'd do it more quickly, circle the rocks until we had to break for cover and then put a slug between our shoulders.

There was no danger at the moment, not while he had his gun under his arm. 'Take a look, Beryl,' I said. 'D'you recognize that guy? That's the fella who's been trying to kill ya. D'you recognize him, d'you know anything about him?'

Cautiously she peeped around the rock, breasts heaving as she panted. Her brow crinkled. 'It's hard to say, now he's all muffled up like that. I can't see his face on account of the goggles. But it doesn't look like anyone I know.'

'He's gonna stalk us down,' I told her. 'He's gonna kill us.'

'We'll fight him,' she said bravely. 'If I can get to the plane, I'll get my gun and ...' She broke off, stared at me. 'You've got it!' she said. 'You've got my gun.'

'That's right,' I said grimly. 'It's right here in my pocket.'

'Give it to me,' she said, eyes flashing. 'I'll go out there and show him.'

I chuckled. 'You're a silly, crazy little dope. But how kissable.' I put my arm around her, showed how I liked her.

'Are you crazy, Hank?' she protested irritably as she pushed me away. 'At a time like this!'

I stepped out from behind the rock, stood in full view of him. I had nothing to worry about. It would take him time to get that gun levelled. He'd seen me all right, but gave no sign, instead was walking steadily towards us.

'For heaven's sake, Hank,' she said fiercely. 'Give me that gun, will you? Any guy who takes a shot at me is gonna get one right back.'

I still stood where I was, in full view of him so he could watch me. 'Listen, stupid,' I said from the corner of my mouth. 'Get this between your ears. That fella's got a rifle. We've got a *revolver*! D'you know how reliable a revolver is? If you don't, as it seems you don't, I'll tell you. It's good for work at close range. You can swing up a revolver and blast with it more quickly than you can a rifle. But right now, that guy's close enough to pick us off with ease, whereas with a revolver I'd use all the bullets and not hit him once at this distance.'

She said: 'Oh!'

'Oh!' I mocked.

She said angrily: 'I could slap your face for talking to me that way.'

'If you wanna live to do any face-slapping, you'd better do what I tell you,' I rasped. 'Step out here in the open, step out alongside me. Stand where he can see us. And when I tell you, raise your hands above your head.'

'What the hell you gonna ...?'

'Do what I say,' I rasped angrily.

I'd never used that tone to her before. She took it, meekly stepped out from behind the rock, stood beside me.

'Now listen to me carefully,' I gritted. 'Keep looking at him. The moment he lifts that gun, jump behind the rocks. Don't waste a moment, just dive behind the rocks.'

'What are you going to do?' she asked.

'Don't worry about me,' I said. 'All I'm concerned with is lulling him into a false sense of security. You stand here, raise your hands in the air when I tell you, and hope like hell he's gonna be fool enough to get within range of my revolver. That'll give us an even chance, gun for gun.'

'Don't do anything crazy, Hank,' she said softly. 'I couldn't bear it. Don't do anything crazy.'

'Just keep your eyes on him,' I said. 'Just get ready to jump.'

He was a cool customer. He was strolling towards us, gun under arm, confidently and unhurried. I watched him as he got closer and closer, becoming identifiable as a tallish guy with broad shoulders. Muffled up in flying jacket and helmet, he musta been sweating like he was in a Turkish bath. But that didn't make him any more hurried. He was gonna kill us. He was gonna kill us as methodically and as surely as a guy hunting down a wounded animal.

'D'you recognize him yet?' I asked Beryl, from the side of my mouth.

'Don't think I've ever seen him before.'

It looked like he was getting within range of my revolver now. I wanted to give him more confidence. 'Raise your hands,' I told her.

We raised our hands. I only half-raised mine, like I hadn't the strength to raise them higher.

He came on towards us, as slowly and as methodically as a robot. He was really close now, almost within uncertain range of my revolver.

'Be careful, Hank,' she whispered. 'Do be careful, honey. I couldn't bear it if ...'

'Get ready to jump,' I gritted. I was gauging all the time with my eyes. He was just about within range now. But I couldn't aim with any certainty. There were so many things to contend with. The trajectory of the bullet; the expansion of the gun muzzle caused by the heat might affect my aim. With luck, I just might be able to hit him even at this distance.

But he was coming closer, with slow, leisurely paces. My heart leaped with hope, because suddenly it seemed he would go on walking until he was well within revolver range. And then, as methodically as he had been walking, he slipped the gun from under his arm, began to level it. It happened so naturally and confidently that his movement was well started before I realized it.

'Jump,' I yelled at Beryl. 'Jump!' And at the same time, I went for the revolver in my trouser pocket. There was no time to jerk it free. The rifle was coming up to his shoulder, would be levelled in a second.

My finger curled around the trigger as I dropped to one knee. I levelled the gun blindly, fired through my pocket, and felt the heat of the bullet as it zipped alongside my thigh. As he cuddled his cheek against the rifle butt, swung the barrel to cover me, the slug hit him.

It was the luckiest shot a guy ever made. And he was the most surprised guy I've ever seen. He gave a shout of pain as the bullet tore into his thigh, spun him off balance, half-falling, half-rolling on the ground.

But even as he hit the ground, the instinct of self-preservation was working inside him. He kept a grip on his rifle, pointed it without sighting, squeezed off slugs that spattered the rock beside me, ricocheting bullets screaming over my head with the ominous wail of death.

I threw another slug at him, which at that distance musta gone well wide of the mark, and jumped madly for the shelter of the rock.

Although we were both out of sight behind the rock, he fired three more times, the bullets chipping rock, screaming overhead like high-pitched jet planes, the echo of the shots rolling around us like thunder.

Then there was silence.

It got me worried. Maybe he was creeping up on us. I risked a quick glance around the side of the rock, and he was limping away, half-stumbling as he clasped his wounded leg.

I sighted carefully, hoped my slug would hit him in the leg, instead of between the shoulders.

I needn't have worried. He was already almost beyond range. Another dozen paces and I could have loosed shots all day at him and never hit him once.

He knew that. At a safe distance he sat down, reloaded his rifle and then, with frequent glances towards us, began to slit open his breeches.

He was hurt bad. Even from that distance I could tell it from the red that soaked his underclothing.

I stepped out from behind the rock, watched him openly. Beryl came out, stood beside me. He kept glancing up at us angrily, as he bound a handkerchief around the upper part of his thigh, used a pencil or some similar-shaped object to insert between the handkerchief and the flesh so he could turn it and form a home-made tourniquet.

'I've a good mind to go over and nail him right now,' gritted Beryl. 'He's a sitting duck.'

'We're the sitting ducks,' I told her. And, as though to

confirm what I said, he picked up the rifle, sighted with it.

We ducked back behind the rock, listened to the sound of lead creasing stone.

'It's stalemate,' I told her. 'He can't get within range of us without being shot. On the other hand, he can't shoot us until he gets really close, unless we're careless.'

'But he's wounded,' she pointed out.

'Yeah,' I agreed thoughtfully. 'That's right. He's wounded.'

'He's lost blood,' she said. 'In this heat, he'll get sick. Then he won't be on his guard against us.'

'Yeah,' I agreed. 'That's right.'

I was figuring other things too. I was remembering our water supply was in the plane and our stores were in the shack. We were caught out there beneath the blistering sun with only two rocks between us and death. If it was a question of waiting, I figured this unknown killer, with the water supply and the shelter of the shack as protection from the burning sun, had a far, far better chance than us, despite his wound.

'I've got an idea,' she said.

'Yeah?'

'He's almost as far from his plane as we are. If we make a sudden, quick dash, we might even get there.'

'Got any more crazy ideas?'

I caught her eyes then. She was smart. She knew what we were up against. She knew that sooner or later the broiling sun was gonna boil our brains in our skulls, that our skin was gonna be burnt and shrivelled from our backs by the hot sun, that we were soon gonna be burnt up and gasping for water.

'We could try it if the worst comes to the worst, anyhow,' she said quietly.

13

We'd been there for an hour. An hour of torture with the sun blistering our limbs, burning through our clothing.

But it was stalemate.

Twice he'd tried to circle around us, approach us from the rear. But he'd soon dropped that idea. It was agony for him to walk, and it was easy for us to circle round the rocks and keep them between us as a barrier.

There was only one way he could get us. Walk right in close and use his rifle. Otherwise he had to play the waiting game.

My revolver was a good argument for keeping him at a distance. And the waiting game was getting him as much as it was getting us.

We watched him all the time now. It was a strain on our eyes, watching him through the white, shimmering heat.

But we couldn't take chances, allow him to come up on us by surprise.

'What's he doing?' asked Beryl.

'His leg's bad,' I told her. 'It's giving him real trouble. He's just taken the tourniquet off, and it's still bleeding. In this heat, his blood's thin, he can't stop the bleeding.'

'This is getting me, Hank,' she panted. 'I feel like a lizard staked out in the sun, slowly shrivelling up.'

'Either he or we have got to break first,' I told her. 'Maybe he'll go into the shack. If he does, that'll give us a chance. We can make a break for the plane, I'll distract his attention by running in close to the shack and using the revolver.'

'Go with me, Hank,' she pleaded. 'I don't want you to do anything crazy.'

'We'd never make it,' I said. 'He'd pick us off easily. We'd never get there.'

'Stick it out here a bit longer, then.'

Another half-an-hour crawled past beneath the blistering heat. Beryl was taking a spell at watching him. 'Quick, Hank,' she breathed. 'Something's happening.'

We stood in the lee of the rocks, watching him as he painfully hobbled towards the shack. He continually glanced over his shoulder at us to make sure we weren't leaving the shelter of the rocks.

'This is maybe our chance,' I breathed.

'Wait a minute, Hank,' she said, hand holding my arm anxiously. 'Let's see what he does.'

It was puzzling. He'd found Beryl's oil-soaked clothes. Limping very badly now, and obviously in great pain, he carried some of them across to the shack, threw them on the ground against the door, bent over them.

I couldn't see what he was doing, but a spiral of smoke and a sudden lick of flame told all we needed to know.

'He's burning down the shack,' said Beryl. 'Why's he doing that?'

'I don't know,' I said grimly. I had the feeling this meant something particularly unpleasant for us.

He was limping towards our plane now, carrying what was left of Beryl's oil-soaked clothing. Beryl realized at the same time as me what was in his mind. She made a swift, impulsive rush towards him. I clutched at her, missed, leaped after her, caught her by the wrist as the unknown killer glanced over his shoulder at us, turned and awkwardly fumbled his rifle to his shoulder.

I got her back behind the rocks as the familiar sound of spattering rock and lead accompanied the shattering vibrations of rifle shots.

She was struggling like a crazy woman. 'I've got to stop him,' she yelled. 'That's my plane. He mustn't burn it. I've gotta stop him. Let me go. I've gotta stop him.'

Maybe she was half crazy from the sun. I had to use my full weight, pin her on the ground, straddle myself across her. She struggled desperately, shrieked aloud, and all the time I was scared, scared that now I wasn't watching him, he'd come up on us, surprise us unprepared.

'Listen to me, honey,' I pleaded. 'You can't go out there. It's sure death. You wouldn't get within a hundred yards of him. He'd put a slug clean through you.'

She was still struggling furiously, frantically. 'I've gotta stop him. He can't do it. I can't let him do it.'

I hated to do it, but common sense had to be shocked into her. I slapped the palm of my hand hard across her cheek, felt the pain of it inside me as she cut short her screaming. She tensed all over. I tensed too, prepared for even more violent struggles. But instead she seemed to collapse, go weak and flabby like a jelly. Her eyes were closed and a tear crawled diagonally across her cheek.

It was safe to leave her, I judged. I got up quickly, peered around the rock. We weren't in any danger. He'd been too busy setting the plane alight. And that oil-soaked clothing in the cockpit was all that was needed. Already flames were shooting upwards, and through the billowing smoke I could see the killer stumbling painfully, very, very slowly along the runway towards his distant plane.

I turned back to Beryl. 'I think he's going,' I said.

She swallowed. 'Did he ...?'

'Yeah,' I said.

I saw her hands clenching tightly together. 'The swine,' she breathed. 'The filthy swine.'

It was interesting. This guy had made four or five attempts to kill her. But she'd never been really upset by him until he'd fired her plane.

'You've got plenty of dough,' I said. 'Why worry about a plane?'

'It's my plane,' she said fiercely. 'I know that plane, love it. It was something that was peculiarly mine.' She suppressed a sob. 'What's the use of trying to tell you. You wouldn't understand.'

'Maybe not,' I said.

'Where's he going?'

I peered around the rock, stood out away from it, shaded my eyes with my hands. Yeah, there was no doubt about it. He was making for his plane. That meant one of two things. Either, having eliminated what little shelter we had, he was now crazy enough to try shooting us from the air, or else ...

'What's the chance of a guy shooting us from the air?' I asked.

'With a rifle?' she asked scornfully. 'Be your age.'

'It's his leg then,' I said. 'He's losing blood, can't stop it bleeding. He's going to get medical assistance.'

'I could kill him, Hank,' she said quietly. 'I wouldn't hesitate. If I had the opportunity, I'd kill him.'

I sat down beside her, turned her around so her head nestled in my lap. 'Don't take it so hard, honey,' I soothed. 'This isn't the end of the world.'

'I know, Hank,' she whispered. 'But it's like losing an old friend.'

I got up from time to time, watched him until he climbed into the cockpit, listened to the roar of the plane. He taxied the full length of the runway, turned around, revved up his engine and then hurtled off into the wind. It was a long while before he was airborne, his wheels leaving the ground just before he reached a rough stretch of scrub. The plane climbed slowly. Maybe it was on account of the heat and the hot air, or maybe on account of his injured leg.

Beryl had got up now, was watching with me. When he was almost out of sight, the unknown killer turned at right angles, banked in a wide circle and set off at a tangent in a straight line.

We watched him until he was out of sight. 'He's gone,' I said.

There was a sudden whoosh, a huge tongue of shooting flame and a hollow boom as the remaining petrol in her plane caught alight.

'That's the end of my plane,' she said, and she was swallowing a lump in her throat.

'I can't figure it,' I said. 'The guy came here to kill us. Yet he hasn't finished the job.'

'It's probably what you said. He's worried about his leg. After all, he doesn't want to kill himself as well.'

'But why burn the plane? Why burn the shack?'

'Wants to make it as tough for us as possible, I guess.'

The sun was beating on the top of my head. I needed shade, coolness, and I needed a drink. And then I got it. We were sixty miles from anywhere, without protection from the sun and without food and water.

I gripped her by the shoulders, turned her around to face me. 'Listen, honey,' I said. 'You remember that crack you made yesterday about walking to the nearest town?'

She was as smart on the uptake as me. 'You think we can make it?' she asked.

'There's no water,' I told her. 'No food.'

'Makes it kinda tough, doesn't it, Hank?'

'It's the only way,' I said. 'That, or stop here until we die of thirst.'

'If the plane hadn't been burnt we'd have had a compass,' she said, putting her finger on a minor but important problem. 'Because how in hell can we reach civilisation if we can't walk in a straight line?'

I looked at her anxiously. I'd heard of folk who'd been lost in the desert, walked around in circles until they dropped from exhaustion. 'Any chance you can remember landmarks?'

Her eyes twinkled mischievously. 'You forget I'm a pilot. Pilots have to learn navigation, you know. I follow a course by the stars.'

'What do we do during the day?' I said irritably. 'Sit down and sunbathe?'

She reached out for my hand. It was the one with my wristwatch. 'Here's a lesson in simple navigation, Bighead,' she said teasingly. 'To find a line running North and South, take a watch, point the hour hand towards the sun and draw an imaginary line midway between the hour hand and twelve o'clock. That line runs North and South.'

'You're not kidding?'

'Even Boy Scouts know it.'

'Maybe there's a chance then,' I said. 'Maybe we'll make it.'

'Of course we'll make it,' she said confidently.

Sixty miles to the nearest town, no food, no water and our feet the only means of locomotion. And all the time that infernal sun blazing down, burning into us, eating us, drying up our blood and sapping our strength.

We talked when we first started, walked side by side, tried to pretend it was just a long stroll. But the sun got so hot it made us giddy, made us weak so that we stumbled, dragged out feet over the hard, sun-cracked, gritty earth. All round as far as the eye could see was a shimmering expanse of sun-dried earth with occasional, sparse patches of desert scrub that somehow managed to exist in this wilderness.

It was after the first ten miles that I realized what was Beryl's greatest trouble. Sure, walking in that heat was bad enough. She was thirsty the way I was, lips and tongue like dried leather. But her real trouble was the burning sun. With only my jacket over her underclothing, there was nothing to cover her slim legs. Already, even in the bright sunlight, they were reddish and sore-looking.

I wanted her to take my shirt to cover herself, but she refused, said I must protect my shoulders, deliberately dropped it on the ground when I draped it around her. Said she'd never wear it, would leave it lying there rather than wear it.

I tried walking behind her to keep her in my shadow. But the sun seemed to be everywhere, beating down on us from directly above.

We stumbled on, wordless now, heads hanging and aching, minds dazed, barely conscious we were walking, and obstinately placing one foot in front of the other with an effort as though the ground was sucking at our shoes. From time to time we checked our bearings, realized that without my watch we'd have been completely lost in that wasteland.

Somehow we kept going all day, kept putting one foot in front of the other until that torturing sun made its swift descent beyond the horizon. Then, like a soothing, liquid stream, coolness enveloped us, gave relief to our parched bodies.

We rested for a while. Our first rest, because it would have been agony to have rested beneath that burning sun. But we made it a short rest, because we could make more rapid progress in the coolness of the night when the sun was not sapping the strength from us.

We walked, we walked and we walked. The sharp cold came down upon us, making walking almost a necessity. Yet because nature must have her way, we rested twice, each time for an hour or more, huddled together for warmth, snatching a little sleep, only to be goaded to our feet again by the frozen numbness of our limbs. Once, we came across a patch of scrubland that was thicker than anywhere we'd come across, and like pigs rooting in a manure heap we went down on hands and knees, sucked at the dry, brown-green grass for the tiny drops of dew that would moisten our parched mouths.

It musta been a coupla hours before dawn when we took our last rest, slept the sleep of exhaustion, our arms around each other and huddled closely together for warmth.

Then like a flash it was day again, with the sun beating down on us, gloating at the torture we were yet to endure.

Our feet were sore and blistered, our voices mere croaks, our strength sapped so it needed an effort to climb to our feet. Yet, so strong is the desire to live within man, that we staggered on, having accomplished so much, determined to accomplish even more.

I figured we'd covered maybe thirty miles or more by this time. But that was as nothing compared with the next ten miles of torture.

It was misery. Sheer, horrible, walking misery. Everything was blurred, time crawling on hot, heavy feet that trailed in the dust, unwilling to move.

My face was blistered by the sun, my eyes narrowed to slits, my vision fuzzy and my head heavy, perpetually dragging me down towards the ground. But incredibly I was still moving forward, one foot after the other, my tongue choking me, cracked and swollen, horrible in my mouth, like a withered and dried-up piece of leather.

In spite of her slimness, she was one of the toughest dames I've ever met. She kept up with me until a coupla hours before sundown. Then, when she went down on her knees, she didn't even call to me. I'd travelled almost a hundred yards before I realized she wasn't with me and turned back.

She was lying there with eyes closed and the tip of her black tongue protruding from the corner of her mouth. I shook her by the shoulder.

'I can't, Hank,' she croaked. 'Go on. Leave me.'

'You've gotta,' I insisted. 'You've gotta.'

'Go on ... you can ... make it alone.'

Two hours to sundown! If I could keep her moving until sundown, we'd have a chance.

The backs of her thighs were dreadful to see, blistered by the sun, the skin peeling away in shreds. She was in no state to protest. I stripped off my shirt, tucked it into the waistband of her briefs so it hung down protectively.

The toughest part was getting her to her feet. I hardly had the strength to stand erect myself. But somehow I managed it, looped her arm around my neck, held on to her wrist and put my other arm around her waist.

It was a nightmare of which I remember little. It was a nightmare of wading through thick, waist-deep mud, my limbs screeching a protest, my muscles aching and groaning, longing to relax with exhaustion, while all the time her dead weight dragged me down towards the ground.

I staggered on, half blind, burnt out and probably half crazy. When the world became dark, I wasn't sure if it was the nightmare that still had me in its grip. Only when the sharp cold caused me to shiver did I awake, realised I was lying with Beryl in my arms and my tired limbs numbed with cold as well as with exhaustion.

I took off her shoes, rubbed life into her numbed toes and blistered feet, warming myself at the same time with the exertion of it. She moaned, and I rubbed her hands, smoothed her hair from her forehead, grunted, groaned and winced with the agony of forcing my own aching limbs into motion and the strain of lifting her once more to her feet.

Then it was on, on, on through the night. On, on, on into the nightmare, with Beryl moaning and protesting I should let her rest, the agony of movement numbing me to my eyes, and the bright stars piercing down at me from a cold, black sky.

On and on into the nightmare of night and misery, weight and drag, carrying and suffering.

The stars piercing down, glittering bewilderingly, revolving around inside my brain, one of them deceptively close, mocking me, winking at me, appearing always nearer and nearer and yet farther and farther, until my crazy mind was reaching for it, my straining body driven towards it by some unrecognized impulse.

It was dancing before my eyes now, getting bigger and bigger, huge and enormous, blocking my entire vision, so that at last, with a surge of exultation, I lunged at it, felt my fist jar on something hard that suddenly gave, heard the tinkling of bells and the sharpness of a knife against my wrist.

The next second, a rectangle of light sprang out to the right of me, the shadowy, looming figure of a man peered through the darkness towards me, and a harsh voice demanded: 'What the hell d'you mean by smashing my window?'

I was on the ground now, Beryl a dead weight lying across my legs.

'Water,' I croaked. 'Water.'

14

He was a tall man, the tallest man I've ever seen. He was thin, too, probably the thinnest man I've ever seen. He stood over me as I slumped in his chair, and his black eyes were heavy with suspicion, his long face melancholy but watchful.

'What d'ya mean, car accident?' he demanded.

I was tired, exhausted. I reached for the enamel mug of water, sipped it, felt the leather fibres of my tongue and mouth absorb the moisture like blotting paper and slowly soften. I wanted sleep. There was nothing I wanted except sleep. My thirst no longer tormented me, but my body ached intolerably and my eyes wouldn't stay open.

He glanced across the shack to the bunk where Beryl lay, half-consciously moaning as the tall man's wife gently applied soothing ointment to her shockingly sun-blistered limbs.

'Ran off the road,' I mumbled, dimly conscious the real story was too crazy to tell. 'Had to walk the rest of the way.'

'How come the dame's got no clothes?' he demanded triumphantly.

'Leave him alone, Jake,' said the woman. 'He's done tuckered up. And lord knows how far they've walked. This poor girl's shoes are worn through, poor thing, feet blistered terribly, must be in agony.'

'I don't rightly like this,' drawled the tall man. He took a plug of tobacco from his pocket, thrust it between his teeth, tore off a chaw and munched steadily, watching me closely meanwhile.

Weakly I nodded towards Beryl. 'Look after her,' I said weakly. 'She's ... all in ... I guess.'

The tall guy nodded, sucked in his cheeks, turned his head aside to deluge a spittoon with brown tobacco juice. Then he glanced across to the far side of the shack, where three boys in their teens wearing hickory shirts and velveteen trousers were watching with wide, suspicious eyes.

'Get the station wagon out, Henry,' said the tall man.

Henry was the tallest boy. His father's word was law. Silently and obediently he crossed to the door, went out into the blackness of the night.

'We just want to rest up awhile,' I said faintly. 'Then we'll be on our way.'

The tall man nodded. 'Sure,' he said. 'Rest a while.'

I half-closed my eyes.

'She's walked her feet near off, poor thing,' said the woman.

I closed my eyes.

'Reckon you're right,' said the man. 'Them's all in.'

I slept.

The grip on my shoulder was steely, the shaking rough and vigorous. I opened my eyes, suppressed a groan of pain as all my body became a conscious ache.

'Snap out of it,' growled a harsh voice. 'Snap out of it, will ya?'

I opened my eyes, stared up at a red face crowned by a light grey stetson. My eyes slipped down across the khaki shirt to the five-pointed star with the word 'Sheriff' embossed on it.

'Up you get, fella,' he rasped. 'Time to get moving.'

I sat up, shook my head dazedly, glanced around the shack to get my bearings.

The Sheriff wasn't alone. He had a deputy and two uniformed State policemen with him. The tall man lounged against the doorpost chewing tobacco. The three boys in hickory shirts were outside the shack with their noses pressed up against the window. One of the panes was broken, I noticed. Then my eyes slipped across the shack to the bunk where Beryl sat with half-closed eyes, head falling on one side like she was so drugged with sleep and exhaustion she couldn't snap out of it. The tall man's wife had her arms around Beryl's shoulders, was talking to her soothingly, offering womanly advice. The woman had turned out her wardrobe, had draped Beryl in a loose-necked, over-large blouse, and a faded black skirt that had to be overlapped, pinned around Beryl's waist with a big safety pin.

The Sheriff took me by the arm, urged me to my feet. 'Come on, fella,' he growled. 'Let's go.'

I wasn't very clear about what was happening. We were outside the shack now, the Sheriff holding my arm, guiding me. The two county cops had Beryl between them, were handling her very gently.

Then we were all in a big, cream car, and it was cramped and the sun was blinding down again, baking us in the interior of the car. But the road was good and solid beneath the tyres and there were other cars on the road, proof that we were near civilisation.

'Where are we going?' I mumbled.

The Sheriff thrust his red face close to mine. 'What's that?' he demanded.

'Where are we going?' I mumbled.

'New Bolton,' he grunted.

'How far?' I muttered.

'Four miles,' he said shortly.

'Jeepers!'

'What's that?'

'Fifty-six miles,' I told him. I was marvelling at it. 'Can you beat that? Fifty-six miles.'

He caught the eyes of one of the county cops, shrugged his shoulders significantly. 'Crazy as a bat,' he muttered.

I dozed.

A rough hand was on my shoulder, shaking me. They were

urging me out of the car. I stood stupidly, watched sleepily as they tried to rouse Beryl. She was drugged with exhaustion, didn't want to move. The county cops decided to carry her.

It wasn't their fault. They couldn't have known about those terribly blistered legs. The touch of their hands as they lifted musta been hellish agony. She screamed, writhed in their grip and, as it seemed she would fall to the ground, one of them clasped her, wrapped his arms around her to save her fall.

It wasn't his fault. After all, when a guy clutches a dame under such circumstances, he's liable to clutch her almost any place.

Beryl's eyes opened. She saw uniforms and felt their hands. A spark of her defiant, cop-hating spirit momentarily flashed. She slapped and struggled, moaned: 'Leave me alone, you mauling swine.'

'Take it easy, lady.'

'Take your mauling hands off me.'

'Just hold her by the arm,' said the Sheriff. 'Get her inside quickly.'

Two hour's sleep I'd had, maybe, in Jake's shack. Dawn wasn't far behind us. My head, my eyes and my body yearned desperately for sleep. I stumbled up the steps of police headquarters, grateful for the Sheriff's helping arm, wondered how I could keep on my feet as they steered me along stone corridors and sighed with gratefulness when I saw the neat, grey-blanketed cot. I didn't care that it was a cell or that cops were helping me onto it.

I slept.

It was the same red-faced Sheriff, but now I could see him with different eyes. I was refreshed, fed and rested. He placed his red hands on the desk and kept his head lowered so his stetson threw a shadow over his eyes. The electric light above blazed down, light-giving but heatless. A constant reminder of the torture I'd endured beneath the sun.

A constant but painless reminder.

'Figured it would be best to let you sleep it off,' he said, with almost a note of apology in his voice.

'I sure needed that rest,' I told him.

He jerked a pack of cigarettes from his pocket, extended them towards me. 'Smoke?'

I thanked him, lit up. There was the deputy lounging against the old-fashioned pipe stove in the corner and two State cops in uniform lounging at the door.

'Had to find out about you,' he said.

'Naturally.'

He opened his desk drawer, pulled out my wallet, opened it up so I could see my press card.

'This yours?'

I nodded.

'You're a *Chicago Chronicle* reporter?'

'That's right.'

'Can you prove it?'

I nodded towards the end of his desk. 'You've got a phone. Ring my office, ask for the Editor. He'll speak to me, confirm it.'

'We'll do just that,' he said.

'Good.'

'One other thing,' he said. 'About the dame. Who is she?'

I was thinking quickly. 'Who does she say she is?' I said cautiously.

'She won't talk,' he said sourly. 'Refuses to give her name, refuses to say anything about herself.'

A germ of an idea was stirring deep down in my mind. She'd been through so much. I didn't want her to suffer any more. I was scared. Scared the killer might be crazy enough to try again, even if it meant capture. Even a coupla days, even one day might make all the difference.

'I haven't the faintest idea who she is,' I told him.

He raised his eyebrows. 'Maybe you'd better do some talking, son,' he said. 'That trader claims you punched a hole in his window, collapsed on his doorstep with the dame naked as the day she was born and you dressed the way you are, just in your trousers. He figured both of you musta escaped from the nut factory over at Crawford.'

'The whole set-up is screwy,' I told him frankly. 'I can hardly believe it myself. I hardly like to tell it you.'

'Try me,' he suggested.

'It's that girl,' I said. 'I think she must be crazy.'

'Tell me,' he encouraged.

'She's a dame I picked up in Chicago,' I told him. 'You know, a pick-up in a bar.'

He nodded wisely.

'We got talking, had a couple of drinks together, and then she invited me to her club.' I paused, added significantly: 'It was a flying club.'

He didn't seem impressed.

I went on. 'She took me for a ride,' I said. 'In an aeroplane. Her aeroplane.'

His eyebrows lifted. I'd got his interest now.

The deputy straightened up, leaned forward interestedly. The two uniformed cops at the door kinda tensed.

'She musta been crazy,' I continued. 'She flew all the way down here from Chicago non-stop, wouldn't land, kept laughing in my face when I pleaded with her to land. Finally she ran out of petrol, had to make a forced landing fifty miles or more from here.'

The Sheriff's eyes were hard and suspicious. Those of the deputy were frankly disbelieving.

I licked my lips, plunged on. 'First thing she did when we landed was to tear off her clothes. I tried to stop her, but she was as scrappy as a wildcat.'

The deputy's mouth moved. I thought I heard the words: 'I bet you tried to stop her,' hanging on the air.

The Sheriff glanced at him coldly, then looked back at me.

'I was in a spot,' I said. 'I didn't know where we were, how to get away from there. And then the craziest of all things happened. She set the plane on fire.'

There was a long silence.

The Sheriff broke it. 'What happened then?'

'You figure it for yourself,' I said. 'You know what it's like out there, sun burning down, no shade, no shelter, no water and no food. There was only one way to get anywhere, and that was to walk. I had to drag her along with me, half-crazy, struggling all the time.' I took out my handkerchief, mopped my forehead. 'I was almost all in when I hit that tall guy's shack. If it hadn't been for finding him, maybe we'd be out there now, being withered by the sun.'

His hard eyes were piercing and unemotional.

The deputy said smoothly: 'Crawford ain't the only place where they've got a nut-house. Better check with the *Chronicle,* Chief.'

The Sheriff grunted, picked up the phone. He looked at me enquiringly. 'What's the number?'

I told him.

'Long distance,' he asked.

It took a time to go through. I was getting worried in case the chief had left early, trusting one of the other reporters to put the paper to bed.

'Are you Healey?' asked the Sheriff into the phone, and I heaved a sigh of relief as I saw by his face he'd got through to the chief.

'Can you describe a guy named Hank Janson?' he asked.

The Sheriff's eyes examined me, checked every detail the chief gave him.

'Can you identify him by voice?' he asked.

Then he passed the phone across to me.

'In trouble again,' sighed the chief down the line.

'Yeah,' I told him. 'Crazy kinda trouble. I wanna get back to town quick. Can you fix it with the Sheriff here? He's a helpful kinda guy. Just check with him I'm not a nut.'

I passed the phone back to the Sheriff. There was maybe a coupla minutes' conversation before he hung up.

'So you really work for the *Chicago Chronicle,*' he said. There was a different note in his voice, one that was almost of awe.

I grinned. 'I'm way off my beat down here.'

He said gently. 'Your Chief wants I should give you every

co-operation. They need you back in town urgent.'

'The police and the press should always co-operate,' I said smoothly.

'What about the dame?' he asked bluntly.

I was getting the Sheriff sized up by this time. 'Hold on to her tight,' I advised. 'Maybe there's a big story here. There's something screwy about a dame who takes up a plane, flies it five hundred miles and then sets it alight.

'You hold on to her. You can figure up some reason, wandering without visible means of support, or begging, or not having a driving licence or some other charge.'

'Indecent exposure,' suggested the deputy.

I glared at him, concentrated on the Sheriff. 'I figure it this way,' I said. 'There's a story here. Whatever it is, it must be big. When it breaks, you fellas down here are gonna get recognition for being smart enough to detain her.'

'What if there's no story?' asked the deputy keenly. 'Supposing she's just a nut?'

'Listen,' I told him. 'Any dame that did what she did is a good story, Nuts or otherwise.'

The Sheriff said artfully: 'You mean the police department here gets a build-up?'

'You played an important part,' I told him.

'I was there too,' said the deputy quickly, suddenly interested.

'Maybe you boys have got photographs,' I suggested gently.

'Come to think of it, I have,' said the Sheriff. 'Had one taken just a year ago. Portrait size it was. Just the thing for ...'

'Get those photos sorted out,' I said urgently. 'The chances are, you'll have photographers down here. But have your own photos handy, in case.'

The Sheriff said with satisfaction: 'The *Chicago Chronicle*'s a real national paper, ain't it? Got more than two million readers they say.'

'More than that,' I assured him. 'More than that.'

'What can we do to help?' he asked.

I grinned ruefully. 'Lend me a shirt and a razor,' I said. 'Is there an airfield near here?'

'There's one over in Crawford,' said the deputy.

'How far's that?'

'Twenty or thirty miles.'

'How do I get there?'

The Sheriff climbed to his feet. 'You go get Mr Janson a shirt. Find him a razor while you're about it.' He reached across the desk, patted me on the shoulder. 'Don't you worry about a thing, son,' he said. 'As soon as you're ready, I'll take you over to Crawford personally in my car.' He put one thumb in his waistcoat armhole. 'If there's one thing the police department down here can pride itself on, it's being helpful and efficient.'

His chest was swelling, his jaw was jutting forward, and in his mind's eye he was already posing for the Chicago photographers.

'And the dame,' I said. 'Don't forget what I said. Keep her safe under lock and key. If she squawks, let her squawk. Keep her here at all costs. Give me three days, and by that time the whole story should break.'

'Rely on us,' he said. 'Rely on us. That's what we're here for. To give service to the public.' He was even preparing his speech.

15

It was a night plane that took me to Chicago, and I slept most of it away. When we landed, dawn was just breaking, I went to the airport canteen, bought myself a good breakfast: coffee, rolls, bacon and eggs and marmalade.

It was seven o'clock when my taxi pulled up outside the Randolph Hotel, and it took five minutes to get Charlie to open up the door of his suite.

He was a very tired and sleepy-looking Charlie, blinking at me through sticky eyelids, enveloped in a red silk dressing-gown. I pushed inside the room, shut the door behind me. 'Snap out of it,' I growled. 'You and me have got to talk serious.'

My hard, urgent attitude snapped life into him. He felt in his dressing-gown pocket for a cigarette. 'Trouble, huh?' he said.

'Lots more than you know,' I said grimly.

'Where's ... Beryl ...?' His eyes were worried; he was almost afraid to frame the question.

'She's safe,' I told him. 'Quite safe where she is.'

He breathed a sigh of relief. 'What went wrong?'

'Who else knew where we were going?' I asked bluntly.

'Why, just you and me,' he said.

'Who else?' I insisted. 'You must have told someone.'

His eyes wouldn't meet mine. 'Maybe I was a bit careless,' he admitted. 'One of the grease monkeys at the airport asked me where the plane was going. I guess maybe I mentioned it.'

'Just like that,' I said bitterly.

'Just like that,' he admitted bleakly.

'He nearly got her.'

His eyebrows raised. 'The killer?'

'We were sitting ducks. He found us by plane, landed, tried to pick us off with his rifle.'

His face went white. 'What happened?'

'I got him in the leg with a revolver. He kept after us for an hour or more, finally had to leave on account of his wound.'

He walked over to a small table, crushed out the stub end of his cigarette slowly. 'What did he look like?' he asked without turning around.

'Never got a look at his face. Wearing flying helmet and goggles all the time.'

'And Beryl? Did she recognize him?'

'Figures she's never seen him before.'

'He seems relentless,' he said worriedly. 'Seems like he's never gonna let up.'

'Beryl's safe where she is now,' I told him. 'Maybe even safer now than she was with me. It's up to us to play this through now, keep those private dicks watching her apartment and keep that substitute sitting duck waiting for him to make one more attempt.

'We've gotta fool him some way, make him think Beryl's back in her apartment, use a substitute for Beryl who's so good he'll make another attempt. It's our only hope. We've got to make him step out of line, walk into our arms.'

He was thoughtful and concerned. 'You leave it all to me,' he said. 'I don't care what it costs. I'll fix this. I'll get busy on it right away.'

'Just don't overlook anything,' I told him.

'You can trust me.' Then his big eyes looked at me soulfully. 'How is she?'

I chuckled. 'Safe as houses. The last place you'd ever guess.'

'Yes?'

'Yeah. She's in jail. We musta looked like a coupla nuts when the cops picked us up. I convinced them who I was, exaggerated about Beryl. You know how she is with cops, hates the sight of them. That helped bolster up my story.'

He chuckled with me. 'I can imagine how mad she is right now,' he said.

'But she's safe,' I pointed out.

'Yes,' he said seriously. 'That's one place he can't get at her.'

'There's one other angle, too,' I told him.

His big eyes studied me solemnly. His eyebrows raised in question.

'The killer's doubled his work now,' I told him. 'He was only after Beryl previously. Now he's gotta get me too. Because I saw him. And one thing he'll never be sure of is if I'll recognize him again.'

'Watch out for yourself, son,' said Charlie.

'That's what I'm always doing.'

He jerked his head towards the cocktail cabinet. 'Have a drink before you go?'

'I'll take a shot.'

'How far did you have to walk?' he asked over the whisky.

I raised my eyes towards the ceiling. 'A nightmare,' I told him. 'Nearly fifty miles.' I took a deep breath. 'We almost didn't make it.'

He nodded sympathetically. 'You almost reached New Bolton?'

'Got to the outskirts,' I told him. 'Hit up with a squatter. He sent his son into town and the cops picked us up.'

He nodded approvingly. 'Smart move that,' he said. 'There's no safer place she can be than in jail.'

'And it's a race between us and the killer now,' I said. 'You've got private dicks working for you, trying to catch him.' I took a deep breath. 'I'm watching out for myself also. Sometime, some place, somewhere, he's gonna take a crack at me too.'

'Watch out for yourself, son,' he warned again. 'Watch out.'

My body was still one vast ache. I'd had breakfast and it was early. It'd be some time before the office opened.

I went to the steam baths, wallowed in hot baths, relaxed in the steam rooms while the aches and weariness of my limbs was soothed away. I came through from the steam-room, settled comfortably on a white cot, called for coffee and the morning papers.

Those steam baths were a wonderful tonic. When I left, I felt fresh and fit, almost a new man. But now I was acting with caution, waiting, tensed inside like an uncoiled spring.

I didn't know who the killer was, I didn't know where he was likely to be. I just had to carry on normally, wait for him to come to me.

I went to the office, went through the morning mail, proof-read the midday edition, took coffee as usual with Charlie Lester, the political correspondent, and wrote a couple of short paragraphs on two shootings on West Side.

I went out to lunch at my usual place, kept my eyes skinned, had cold shivers down my spine all the time, expecting, even hoping, that something would happen.

I got back from lunch, and there was a lull in the work. I kept thinking of Beryl, wondered how she was making out. Finally I realized how simple it would be to find out. I told the operator to get me the Sheriff's Office at New Bolton.

It took half-an-hour to get through!

'This is Janson here ...' I began.

He almost jumped down the phone at me. 'I'm writing a-full report for the DA,' he snarled. 'Perjury and libel, that's what it was. And if you ever put your foot inside city limits here ...'

'What's happened?' I interrupted tersely. 'What's biting you?'

'The dame,' he snarled. 'The dame you told me was nuts. I've got four lawyers sitting in the outer office, all of them waiting to serve writs on me. I'm being threatened with suspension, served with writs for kidnapping, for illegal detention and the dame's got all the money in the world.

Seems like she's gonna spend every penny of it to ease me out of my job.'

'You dope,' I said furiously. 'Why did you let her talk to anybody? Why did you let her see anyone?'

He almost exploded. 'Talk! If anyone's been doing the talking it wasn't me. She didn't talk to anyone. This battery of legal eagles descended on me like an avalanche. I had to spring her at once. They're putting a pair of skids under my office chair right now. I'm gonna be out of a job and ...'

'Wait a minute,' I said urgently. 'Did you say they've sprung her?'

'Sure they sprung her. Fourteen different ways. There's the best legal brains in the State pitted against me and ...'

'This is a matter of life and death,' I said urgently. 'Let me speak to her. I've got to speak to her.'

'Speak to her!' he roared. 'She's in Chicago by now. Caught the train out of here hours ago. Those lawyers had dough for her, even brought clothes along for her.'

I was sweating all over. 'She's caught the train to Chicago,' I echoed. 'How long ago?'

'Hours ago,' he said. 'Probably in town by now.'

'What train did she catch?' I asked faintly. 'What time was it?'

'How the hell do I know?' he roared explosively. 'And what are you going to do about all these legal vultures crowding ...?'

I hung up, reached for the timetable. My hands were shaking as I thumbed through the pages, ran my fingers down over the small type. There was only one train she could have caught. I looked at the arrival time, glanced up at the clock. I had just about ten minutes to get to the station, meet her on the platform.

I'd have made it, too, if there hadn't been a traffic jam. That cost me a valuable three minutes. I raced madly through the station, pushing, thrusting, ignoring the outraged faces of folks I shouldered aside. I reached the platform where the train had come in, and already half the passengers had filed off.

I waited there impatiently, sweating, eyes searching along the platform among the bobbing heads. She might already have left. But she might be among those passengers still handing over their tickets.

She wasn't there. It seemed an age before all the passengers were off the platform. By that time, I was sweating so that I was almost faint with it.

I went off at a run again, rushing across the platform, scattering hurrying passengers as I passed. I caught a taxi, bawled the address at the driver, promised him treble pay if he got there quickly.

He sure did his best. It was more like a Ben Hur chariot race than a taxi ride. He became a demon driver, the most reckless taxi-driver in town. And I loved him like a brother.

I had the door of the cab open before he drew to a halt outside the apartment block. I yelled at him to wait, dashed up the steps three at a time, crashed through the swing doors. The lift was going up. The uniformed commissionaire eyed me curiously.

'Miss Pinder,' I panted. 'Have you seen her?'

He jerked his thumb at the lift. 'Just gone up, sir,' he said. 'The lift will be down in a minute.'

I didn't wait for the elevator. I went up those steps like a madman. There was only one thought in my mind. I had to get to her quickly. I knew it with certainty now. The killer was waiting for her. It had all been planned, all arranged. Everything had been gambled on this last, desperate attempt to kill her.

She musta been only a few seconds ahead of me. I heard the elevator gates slam as I reached the floor below hers. I raced up the last flight like I was training for the Derby stakes, rounded the corner into the corridor, raced to the door of her apartment, which was just closing.

I reached it travelling at about twenty miles an hour, slammed her full across the lobby as the door crashed open beneath my weight.

She stared at me with hard eyes that almost immediately filled with anger. Then, without a second's hesitation, she ran along the corridor towards the lounge.

I knew what was in her mind. She hated me. Hated me as she'd never hated anyone. She musta learned from the Sheriff the part I'd played in her continued confinement. She was really gonna do it this time, phone for the management and have me thrown out.

I went after her, eyes, ears and all my senses pricked and attuned for danger.

I caught her as she reached the lounge. I caught her around the waist, flung her to the floor. Over by the curtained window my searching eyes had caught a flicker of movement.

I went across the room in a rugby tackle, saw the curtains sway while I was in mid air, heard the muffled roar of a gun and the whistle of lead whining over my shoulder. I hit him like a small shell, the two of us rolling on the ground, him enveloped in the curtain and me struggling, reaching for his gun hand. The gun went off again, the scorch of it against my cheek, the flash and sting of cordite in my eyes.

I was boiling, boiling mad. I hammered, pounded at that struggling figure shrouded in the thick velvet curtain until the red haze cleared and I realized I was astride him and he was still, unmoving.

I got to my feet, trembling with emotion, pulled back the curtain, stood staring down at him.

He was a dark guy, stockily built, with bushy eyebrows and a mean little mouth. The gun had fallen from his hand. I picked it up, pocketed it. Then, just to make sure, I bent over him, fingered his thigh.

He was the guy right enough. I could feel the pad of antiseptic gauze beneath the bandages.

Beryl was standing beside me, staring down at him, wide-eyed and white-faced. 'He almost killed you, Hank,' she whispered.

'He almost killed you,' I said grimly.

'But ... how did you know ...? I had no idea. I'd have

walked right in here and ...'

'There's a lot of things you don't know,' I said grimly. 'There's a lot of things you've gotta learn.'

The unknown man stirred uneasily.

'D'you know him?' I asked Beryl.

'Never seen him before,' she said.

I bent over, took him by the collar, jerked him to his feet, dragged him across to an armchair and slammed him down.

He moaned a coupla times, half-opened his eyes.

I went to the cocktail cabinet for a soda-siphon. I sprayed it over him until he spluttered, moved his hands protectively to his face.

I stopped squirting, stood over him with hands on my hips.

He bleared up at me.

'Okay,' I snarled. 'Start talking.'

He glared at me, glared at Beryl. He clamped his lips tightly together, said nothing.

'You know what's coming to you,' I said quietly. 'Attempted murder is a crime that gets you twenty years. That's what's gonna happen to you, fella. Twenty years down the river. You'll be an old man by the time you come out.'

He looked hunted, glanced around quickly and uneasily, as though seeking a means of escape.

I patted my trouser pocket. 'I've got your gun, fella,' I said. 'At this range I can put a bullet through your other leg as easily as dropping a nickel in the phone coinbox.'

He kinda slumped in the chair. But his eyes were glittering balefully.

'You've got one chance, fella,' I told him. 'Twenty years if you take this rap alone. Maybe five or ten years less if you tell everything.'

He clamped his lips tightly together, said nothing.

'Get the cops on the phone, Beryl,' I said.

She hesitated.

'The cops,' I growled. 'Ring Homicide.'

She still hesitated, then she squared her shoulders, made her decision. 'Okay, Hank,' she said quietly. 'I guess we'll have to put up with the cops. But it's worth it to fix a guy who can set fire to a plane.'

I still stood in front of him. He still kept his lips clamped tightly together. 'You've got just a few minutes,' I told him. 'They're on the way now.'

He still kept his lips tightly together.

'Take a good look at him, Beryl. He's a sucker. The world's biggest sucker. He's been played for a fall guy. Now he's gonna take the rap all by himself.'

He was white now, but he still kept his lips glued together.

'You might as well talk, fella,' I said. 'It'll look better if it comes as a confession. The cops are gonna know about it, anyway.'

His eyes were narrowed, watching me craftily.

'What's Charlie to you, anyway?' I said casually.

Beryl tensed. The guy tensed. He sat that way, tensed up for quite a while. Then quite suddenly he relaxed like a tyre collapsing as the air's let out of it. 'How d'you know about him?' he asked.

'Because it had to be him,' I said. 'Because he wasn't being smart enough. Because he was the one guy that knew where I took Beryl in that plane, and the one guy who knew she was in jail. He was the only man who could send lawyers to get her released.'

Beryl's face was white and shocked. 'Charlie!' she echoed. 'What are you talking about? Charlie. What's he got to do with this?'

I nodded towards the unknown guy. 'Ask him,' I said grimly. 'He'll tell you.'

'He talked me into it,' he muttered defensively.

'How much were you gonna get out of it?' I demanded.

He kinda shrank back into the armchair. Maybe the tone of my voice was ugly. 'He was gonna see me okay if I fixed it,' he whispered.

'Sure,' I jeered. 'You just took his word for it. You were real close buddies.'

Just for a moment his eyes flickered defiance. 'He's my

father,' he announced. 'That was good enough, wasn't it?'

'You're lying,' said Beryl. 'He never had any children.'

He looked at her, looked away quickly. 'Maybe he wasn't married to my mother,' he muttered. 'But he's looked after her swell all these years. Many guys would have just deserted her.'

Beryl stared at him, disbelievingly. Then quite suddenly she spun on her heel, walked across the room, stood with her hand on the cocktail cabinet, staring at the wall.

We hadn't closed the door of the apartment behind us. It was open when the cops arrived, and they came right in. They all wore uniforms and they all looked very official.

I tensed, waiting for the explosive reaction that would come from Beryl.

It never came.

'I'd never have got through today without your help,' she whispered.

'It was a shock for you, honey,' I said. 'But you'll get over it. This is a tough world. You've got to learn that almost anything can happen.'

'But Charlie,' she said. 'It's so incredible. I still can't believe it.'

'Forget about it now, honey,' I said soothingly. 'Just let the cops worry about it. It's in their hands now. There's nothing more you can do.'

'But it was so unnecessary, Hank,' she whispered. 'He could have had what he wanted, anything. He must have known that.'

'Maybe he did,' I said. 'But he wanted it all for himself. Maybe he'd have given his son something. Maybe he'd have set him up in a small business somewhere. But when greed gets into guys, there's no stopping them. They go crazy about dough, will do anything for it.'

'It's made me feel all twisted up inside, Hank.'

'Don't think about it, honey,' I soothed. 'Don't think about it.' I soothed her gently in a way that would make her think of other things. It did. She nestled her cheek against mine, held me tightly.

'We've been through a lot together, Hank,' she whispered.

'We sure have, honey.'

'When you do that it gets me so ... oh ... I want to eat you!'

I did it some more.

'Oh, Hank!' she whispered.

She gave a long shuddering sigh.

'Oh, Hank!'

'Honey,' I breathed. 'Jeepers, I want you so badly ...'

She was half-laughing, half-crying. 'Don't you know what it is, Hank? It's so crazy. It seems like there's always something. The other night it was the joy-stick. Now it's ...' She gave a quick sob of pain.

'What is it, honey?'

'My legs, Bighead. They're so painful, red raw. I could almost cry with it.'

'I'll try to be gentle, honey,' I said. 'I'll soothe you. After all, my jacket did keep the sun off your shoulders!'

Other Crime Titles available from Telos Publishing

<u>PRISCILLA MASTERS</u>
WINDING UP THE SERPENT
CATCH THE FALLEN SPARROW
A WREATH FOR MY SISTER
AND NONE SHALL SLEEP
SCARING CROWS
EMBROIDERING SHROUDS

<u>TONY RICHARDS</u>
THE DESERT KEEPS ITS DEAD

<u>HANK JANSON</u>
Classic pulp crime thrillers from the 1940s and 1950s.
TORMENT
WOMEN HATE TILL DEATH
SOME LOOK BETTER DEAD
SKIRTS BRING ME SORROW
WHEN DAMES GET TOUGH
ACCUSED
KILLER
FRAILS CAN BE SO TOUGH
BROADS DON'T SCARE EASY
KILL HER IF YOU CAN
LILIES FOR MY LOVELY
BLONDE ON THE SPOT
THIS WOMAN IS DEATH
THE LADY HAS A SCAR
BABY, DON'T DARE SQUEAL

Non-fiction

THE TRIALS OF HANK JANSON by STEVE HOLLAND

For full details of all Telos titles, please visit our website at
www.telos.co.uk where there are facilities for worldwide
credit card online ordering.